WAR *of the* EAGLES

Eric Walters

ORCA BOOK PUBLISHERS

Canadian Cataloguing in Publication Data
Walters, Eric, 1957-
War of the eagles

ISBN 1-55143-118-1 (bound)   ISBN 1-55143-099-1 (pbk.)
1. Haida Indians — Juvenile fiction. I. Title.
PS8595.A598W37 1998   jC813'.54   C97-911119-6
PZ7.W1713Wa 1998

Library of Congress Catalog Card Number: 97-81084

Orca Book Publishers gratefully acknowledges the support of our publishing programs provided by the following agencies: the Department of Canadian Heritage, The Canada Council for the Arts, and the British Columbia Ministry Arts Council.

Cover painting and design by Ken Campbell
Printed and bound in Canada

Orca Book Publishers   Orca Book Publishers
PO Box 5626, Station B   PO Box 468
Victoria, BC Canada   Custer, WA USA
V8R 6S4   98240-0468

00 99 98   5 4 3 2 1

Dedication

When I was ten years old, I was searching through our old cedar chest and came across a picture of my father, much, much younger, wearing an army uniform and holding an eagle in his outstretched arms. The eagle was dead. I didn't understand how this could be. My father was a tough man, someone who didn't always have a lot of time for people, but he always had time for animals. We never had much money, but if a stray and injured cat wandered by, what money we had would go towards fixing whatever was wrong.

It was unimaginable to me that my father could have killed that eagle. I asked him to tell me what had happened. Reluctantly, he told me a small sliver of a story. Over a period of time, a few more episodes escaped. As it turned out, he was telling me about the most exciting time in his life — the time he spent as a soldier stationed in Prince Rupert during the Second World War.

Almost thirty years later, those fragments inspired this novel. On the day I finished the final draft of *War of the Eagles* my father passed on. He never got the chance to see the finished novel or to read this dedication.

My father taught me a lot in life. Perhaps the most important lesson he taught was the importance of cherishing the events which surround you and of realizing that the "good old days" are happening right now. This novel is for you, Dad.

Dedicated to my father, Eric George Walters. December 7, 1915 — August 28, 1997.

.1.

I felt the weak yellow light from the morning sun, although its face still remained hidden behind the mountain tops. A thick layer of fog clung waist high to the ground, but gathered into deeper pools in the nooks and depressions of the forest floor. The chill in the air felt good as each breath filled my lungs; cool, moist air, scented with the aroma of the trees. The tops of the tallest trees, Douglas firs, red cedars, hemlock and Sitkas, disappeared into the gloom, lost from my view. Below, the small cedars and other evergreens fought amongst themselves to capture whatever sunlight managed to filter through the giants above.

The ground was littered with deadfall and my steps were announced by the cracking and snapping of twigs. Hardly audible, but to the creatures of the forest the sound was a loud cry of warning. Every few steps I would stop ... and listen. Listen. Listen. Moving through the underbrush, my clothes became increasingly damp from the dew clinging to the leaves and needles. Small ferns, moss and fungus were everywhere.

The ground became soft and silent. I was standing on a section of muskeg, one of many extending throughout the forest in places where the water never leaves the ground. This was good. The spongy earth muffled my clumsy footfalls and, for now, I was as noiseless as any other animal. Between the softness under my feet and the white fog floating all around, I imagined I was walking on a cloud.

Both my father and grandfather had been my guides and teachers during earlier morning outings. All their differences were gone when they were out together hunting. We always went out at dawn because that's the best time. The creatures of the night, tired from hunting or being hunted, are less careful before they seek out their refuge from the day. The creatures of the day, not yet completely in their time, are unsure of themselves. Alone on this morning I didn't fear the forest or the animals that lived, and died, within it.

I couldn't help but think of my grandfather. Cradled in my arms was his gun, an old Enfield .303. The wooden handle was worn, the barrel darkened with age, but the sights were true and it shot straight. Straight and true. Like my grandfather. Even when he was old and stooped, he still stood straight and true.

He always said his rifle had a magic spirit which helped guide its bullets to the target. My father didn't believe in such things. He said my grandfather was just "one heck of a shot." I know my father was right, but still, each time I squeezed the trigger I hoped there was magic.

My father was gone too. Gone off to fight a war halfway around the world. He'd be coming back someday, but that didn't make it any easier when I missed him. We'd spent so much time together. Hunting and fishing, flying together in his bush plane, just talking. He'd laugh at me if I ever told him just how much he and my grandfather, my mother's father, were alike. The proud and stubborn Haida, and the proud and stubborn Englishman.

My mother's and grandmother's people were Tsimshians. Both the Tsimshians and Haida believe in many things.

When a Tsimshian dies, if he's led a good life, he comes back to earth as an eagle or a raven or another one of the creatures of the forest or ocean. My father tells me not to believe everything I'm told, not to get caught up in all that "Indian mumbo jumbo." My mother just smiles and says those stories make as much sense as the ones the ministers tell us in church.

Looking up, I caught my first sight of the morning sun peeking through the towering evergreens. The fog and dew were being drawn back up into the sky.

Off to the left I caught a glimpse of movement. I froze in my steps and slowly, ever so slowly, pivoted toward the motion. There, flitting in and out of the bushes and the remaining threads of mist, was a jackrabbit. Fat and satisfied from a night of feeding, it was too content to notice me. In slow motion, I drew the rifle up. The handle felt smooth against my cheek, my finger rested against the trigger. I took aim.

The hare, nibbling on a few more blades of grass, was squarely in my sights. It stopped eating and looked up, right at me. Gentle, soft eyes, so alive, so innocent. I squeezed the trigger and with a deafening noise the bullet flew and ripped through the hare's chest, driving it violently backwards. I lowered the rifle, shouldered it and walked over to pick up the carcass. It had been blown back under a bush. I crouched down and retrieved it, dragging it out by its back legs.

It was long and limp, its soft brown eyes open and vacant. Blood dripped out of the gaping hole where the bullet escaped, making the brown fur sticky and warm. It was a clean kill and I was grateful. The rabbit was dead before it even heard the shot. I opened my canvas sack — my game bag — and put the rabbit in and closed the flap.

Looking around I realized I wasn't completely sure where I was, although that wasn't a problem. The sun was bright and I'd use it as my guide to find the ocean. From there I'd just move north up the coast until I reached our village. It couldn't be much more than a mile.

The trees were now alive with the sounds of birds. My footsteps echoed back at me. I didn't have to move quietly anymore since I'd got my catch for the day. My grandfather always said "Only take what you can use, what you need." His words were so vivid that sometimes, when I closed my eyes, it felt like I could still hear him.

My thoughts were interrupted by a new sound. At first it was so faint it could be taken for the wind blowing through the trees. But as I moved on, it became unmistakable — the ocean. The rhythm of the waves crashed against the shore. The smell of the salt water, always present everywhere on the island, became even more pronounced. I knew it was just through this next bunch of trees, or the next, or the next. Pushing through a clump of cedars I found myself on a thin stretch of stony beach. Only a few yards away the waves were breaking and retreating. I looked around and immediately knew where I was. My grandmother's house was no more than a half mile up the coast, just around the next point.

Down the coast in the other direction I made out the faint outline of another village, Sikima. It had about one hundred families. All Japanese fishermen. My best friend, Tadashi Fukushima, lived there with his family: his parents, two sisters and grandmother. He and I spent a lot of time in each other's homes. It seemed like half the time he ate at my house and the other half, I ate at his.

Since before I could remember we'd always spent all our summers up here with my mother's parents, and Tadashi and I had been friends. Our friendship was one of the few things that made it even a little okay when my mother decided not to return to Victoria after the summer ended. She said, with Dad away in Europe, there really wasn't any point in leaving. This really was my mother's home. She was born and raised here. So was my Naani, and her mother and her mother and her mother. Naani says her people have been here since time began. I once kidded her that that must make this the Garden of Eden. She just smiled and said yes. I didn't care about any of that. I just wanted to go back to my school and my friends and sleep in my bed in my house. There was a big difference between visiting some place and having to live there.

The beach was covered with small, flat rocks just perfect for skipping. If my stomach hadn't been calling me for breakfast I'd have pitched a few. Rounding the point I could clearly see home. It sat amongst two dozen other houses. They were in no particular pattern, just haphazardly placed on little chunks of land skirting the rocky outcrops that are everywhere on the island. The houses were different sizes and shapes but each was bleached white and needed to be painted. Scattered about as they were, they looked like grains of salt dropped from a giant shaker.

Not that I ever would, but I could walk into any of the houses in our village and sit down at the kitchen table. Without a word someone would set another place at the table. Every single person in the whole village is related to me in one way or another. I have trouble figuring it all out, but my grandmother can tell me who is my cousin or great-uncle or whatever. We're all family, all part of the same clan.

On the front porch I saw my grandmother, my Naani. She sat on the steps, a bowl held between her legs, cutting up beans. She nodded at me and a faint smile crept onto her face.

"Any magic, this morning?"

"You tell me there's magic everywhere," I answered, "so why should this morning be any different?"

"I'm glad to hear you listen to my stories."

"I listen to everything my Naani says. That doesn't mean I believe, but I listen."

My grandmother can't read or write. That doesn't stop her from being a storyteller and the keeper of our clan's history. She knows about everything and everybody. People come to listen for hours when she talks. She's almost as good as the radio. Of course, people wouldn't know anything about the radio, since there isn't one in the entire village.

Naani is also a medicine woman. She knows about the herbs and plants growing in the forest. People who aren't feeling well come to see her and she gives them advice and medicines. They treat her the same way people in the towns treat the doctor.

I removed the sack from around my neck and dropped it on her lap. "Here's a little meat for the pot."

She picked up the bag and looked inside. "Very little. Game is all going farther into the forest. All those soldiers driving 'em away."

The game had been a lot more scarce since the soldiers started building their camp.

Before the war everybody always stayed pretty much in Prince Rupert. Now the soldiers had built a road in, cut down trees, dragged in supplies and started putting up buildings. There were lots of soldiers. I heard when it was finished there'd be a whole battalion stationed there. Hard to imagine.

Naani put aside her beans and took the rabbit out of the sack. She pulled a sharp knife out of the sheath hanging around her waist. First, she made circular cuts around each of the four paws. Then, a similar cut around the neck. Next she turned the rabbit over and made a cut, not too deep, along the whole underside. She peeled the skin away from the carcass. The pelt parted from the flesh with a tearing sound.

I was always amazed at how she did it. It was like watching somebody peel a banana. It seemed so effortless. The whitish carcass, ringed with blue veins, was separated from the skin. Within two minutes she'd finished and dropped the entire pelt, all in one piece, to the floor of the porch. It was so perfect you'd think she could sew it back on and send the rabbit on its way.

"Jedidiah, go and get me a couple of pots."

In the short time it took me to go to the kitchen and come back, she'd already started to gut the rabbit. She now had an audience. The two stray cats that lived around our village were sitting in the dirt by the porch, watching her every move. They saw me coming and moved farther away.

"What's with those cats? Why don't they like me?"

She smiled and tossed a small piece of rabbit gut in their direction. They both scrambled after it. "Cats like people who like them."

"What's to like, they're just a couple of cats. Dirty and flea bitten. They're always just here. Who owns them anyway?"

"Nobody. They're cats. Nobody owns cats. For a smart kid you's sometimes not so smart." She tossed two more pieces of rabbit gut to them.

"Here let me give them all the guts," I suggested. "Maybe that'll make me more popular." I liked the meat, not the middle, and figured this was a good way to get rid of the parts I didn't want to find in my stew.

"The guts are the best part. Heart, liver, stomach. Best parts."

She gave me a knowing smile. She knew what I was thinking. It was almost spooky the way she did that, although it explained where my mother got her ability from.

"Yuck!" I answered, scrunching up my face. "Guts are for cats, not for people."

"You may be half native but your belly is full white," she chuckled as she reached over and grabbed my stomach. Her hands were still dripping with rabbit guts and I scrambled away from her hold.

"Tadashi's parents say I eat like I'm Japanese."

"Japanese, white, it don't matter," she said with a twinkle in her eye. "All the same to me. I can't tell one apart from the other. Maybe that's the problem with the grub. I've been cooking the guts. If you have a Japanese stomach you'd probably like it raw, like the fish. Go down by the cats and I'll toss you a couple pieces of guts too."

"You know, old woman," I said, smiling back at her, "I think the hunter should get to choose how the food should be prepared."

"Shows how much you know. The one doing the cooking is the one who's in charge."

When it was just me, my mother and father living together, my mother would cook to please my dad. Meat and potatoes, boiled or steamed. Now, with just me and mom living with her, my Naani had done most of the cooking and I had to learn to eat things I'd never even considered food before. If it swims or floats in the ocean, runs or grows in the forest, my Naani knows how to cook it.

"I'm gonna fix this rabbit up good. Make a stew ... let it simmer all day ... the way your mama liked it when she was a girl. It's good to see all that white food hasn't spoiled her tongue."

"Is Mom coming home tonight?" I knew the answer but wanted reassurance.

"She been gone for four days. Should be back tonight."

My mother worked as a cook up at the new army camp. She worked for four days, then she was off for four days. The four days off were good. The four days she worked were long. With my Naani around, not to mention all my relatives and Tadashi, I was never alone. It was just that I missed her.

It was even harder than having my father gone. Because he was a bush pilot, I was more or less used to him being away, sometimes for months at a time if he was flying for some mining company up north. Of course, if the job was going to last longer, me and mom would join him, rent a house and live in that town. I've lived in little towns in B.C., Alaska and the Yukon. That's one of the reasons I resented us coming up here to live now. Finally for the past two years we'd stayed in one place. I started and finished the year in the same school, got to know some kids and felt like I had a real home for the first time.

The army camp wasn't far away, and sometimes I'd go up and see Mom on her four-day shifts. Lately though, since that new major arrived, it hadn't been as often. He told her it was a military base and "unauthorized civilians" weren't supposed to be snooping around. What did he think I was, a German spy?

Of course, he was partly right. I did spy on what they were doing. Tadashi and I often sat off in the trees and watched the soldiers running around, cutting things down and putting up buildings. Funniest thing I ever saw was them trying to get a jeep out of a bog. By the time they were finished they'd almost lost a second jeep, the one they thought would pull out the first. Little by little, over the past two weeks the jeep had been sinking deeper into the ground. Last time I checked, it was more than half buried. I'd heard they were waiting for the ground to dry up. They didn't know Prince Rupert very well 'cause they were going to wait forever if they were waiting for a dry spell to come.

"I need you to go to Rupert for me and pick up a few things," Naani said.

"Rupert! Sure! Tadashi's coming over this morning and he could come with me. That is if you say it's okay."

"Fine by me. It's better he go with you anyhow. Rupert isn't like it used to be with all them soldiers and government men running 'round. Not so quiet, not so friendly anymore. I don't even like going."

"You never liked going there. Besides, I think it's got better since it got busier."

"Busier yes ... better no," she said. "Something can't be busier and better at the same time. Now listen and I'll tell you what I need."

over this morning
over it's okay
with you anyhow
than soldiers and
to quiet, not so
oing
Besides, I think it's
Something can I
time. Now listen and

.2.

"Prince Rupert, definitely!" Tadashi replied enthusiastically. "My parents don't like me to go there, but if we're doing something for your grandmother then it's okay."

One of the things the Japanese and the Tsimshian share is respect for age. They both figure the older somebody is, the more things they know. If an old person asks you to do something, it's just supposed to be done, no questions asked.

"Are you sure you can remember everything I want?" Naani asked.

"I'm sure, but if you want, I'll write it down."

"Pssshhhh," she said as she puffed air out of her cheeks. "If you have to write it down, it can't be too important, can it? I've gone my whole life without writing anything down. Can you remember?" she added, turning to Tadashi.

"Yes, ma'am," Tadashi replied seriously.

"And you boys be careful."

"We're just going to Rupert, we're not going off to fight the Germans," I chided her.

Tadashi poked me in the ribs. "Yes, ma'am."

"You learn from your friend there. 'Sides, if you get into trouble, you'll wish it was only the Germans who was mad at you," she scolded. "Here, take this bag. I packed a snack and a canteen," she added as she handed me the knapsack.

"Thanks. We better get going."

"First things first. Come, give the old woman a hug. You too, Tadashi."

We both dutifully obeyed. She reached up to put an arm around my shoulder. I remember not so long ago when I was the one who had to reach up when we hugged.

We started down the trail to the woods. It was faster than following the shoreline into town. Just before we disappeared into the forest I heard my Naani yell, "Be good!" I turned and waved goodbye.

For the past three weeks, ever since school began, we traveled along this trail. Tadashi, along with his sisters Midori and Yuri, and all the other kids from his village would pass by our village and would be joined by all of us who were going to school. It was a two-mile walk for them to get as far as us and then almost three more miles to the school on the outskirts of Prince Rupert. Walking along we'd always break into little groups moving through the forest. Tadashi and I always walked together. Usually we had lots to say to each other, but some mornings we just traveled in silence. We were good enough friends that we didn't need to talk. This afternoon, except for a few words, we moved without talking.

Coming around the bend we crossed behind our school. It wasn't much. Certainly not much compared to the schools down south. It was flat, wooden, painted red, one story high, with a tar-covered roof. They had just re-tarred it during the summer. I'd watched them doing it, and stood there taking deep breaths. I love the smell of tar. In Rupert things don't have to be built for warmth but they have to be watertight. I can hardly remember a day here when it didn't at least try to rain or snow.

The curtains on the windows were all closed and it looked lonely and deserted. A rusting set of swings was off to the side. In the back was the sorriest excuse for a baseball field I ever saw. The backstop and the infield weren't bad, but the outfield was pathetic. Bad enough that it was littered with rocks, but it was so tiny. Even a puny eight-year-old could be a hero and belt a homer out into the forest. Games were always being called off because we ran out of balls that had been hit into the forest and disappeared into the ferns and undergrowth.

Rupert was a real baseball town. The kids loved playing ball. Even the Japanese kids, who seemed to have this strange idea that school was only about learning, played ball. Good ball. Tadashi had a "live" arm and usually pitched. He played fair but he didn't mind whistling one up right under your nose if you were crowding the plate. Hard but fair.

The school was on a rise on the edge of the town.

"Quite a sight," Tadashi said, spreading his arms out. "Rupert?"

"Of course, Rupert. It's exciting. Look at all the houses, the stores, ships out in the harbor, cars, streets … people."

"This place?" I laughed. "Compared to Vancouver or Victoria, this is just a little pimple."

"Don't rub it in," he said, his eyes scanning the horizon. "This is the biggest pimple I've ever seen. Someday I'll see more. More than just Victoria or even Vancouver."

"My father says that even Vancouver isn't much compared to other places, places like London. He says Prince Rupert isn't the end of the world but you can see it from here," I said.

My father thinks the center of the world, the center of civilization, is in Europe and the only thing we have that comes close is Victoria, because it's modeled after London. That's why we finally settled there to set up his business, because it reminded him of home. Of course, for my mother, home is Rupert. She says home is wherever you were raised. I was raised in so many places I feel comfortable in lots of them but not really home in any of them.

I once asked my father why he lived in the sticks if he thought civilization was so wonderful. He told me civilization would be just fine if it wasn't for all the damn people.

"I'm not going to spend my whole life on the edge of the world," Tadashi said. "I want to see more, do more than my father. I don't want to be just a fisherman."

"Nothing wrong with being a fisherman."

"Come on, Jed, I didn't say there was. I just want more."

"Plenty of call for doctors everywhere." Tadashi wanted to go into medicine.

"You're right," he nodded. "A doctor is a good thing to be. Lots of money. Lots of opportunity. Lots of respect. It's what my father wants for me."

"You'll be a good doctor. Not that I'd trust you to fix anything of mine," I joked.

"Very reassuring. I just hope my Japanese is good enough to get me through school."

"Your Japanese?"

"Yeah. I'll have to go to Japan to study."

"Why Japan? We got schools here for that sort of thing."

Tadashi shrugged. "Not schools for me. They don't let Japanese into them."

"What do you mean, Japanese? You were born here. Your father is a naturalized Canadian. You're Canadian."

"Yellow skin, slanty dark eyes, dark hair. To some people I can't ever be a Canadian." His voice had gotten quiet and he walked in front of me so our eyes wouldn't meet.

"Tadpole," I called, using the nickname only his sisters and I called him. He turned around. "All that means

· 18 ·

is that some people are stupid. You just wait. Someday you'll be Dr. Tadpole, living in a big city, proud father of five children, owner of a large house and fancy car, and, best of all … married to the lovely Kiyoka.

A smile came to his face and he slowly nodded his head but didn't say a word.

"Come on, enough daydreaming," I teased. "Let's go and see the excitement of Prince Rupert." I started to walk again. I had to admit, at least to myself, that Rupert had certainly become a lot more exciting in the last few years since the war had started.

Prince Rupert sits on the north part of Kaien Island. The island is so close to the mainland that a bridge was built to connect the two. It probably has the best harbor in the world, deep and wide and protected from the winds and currents. A ship in the harbor is as safe as a toy floating in a bathtub. I looked down at the ships at anchor in the harbor and counted over two dozen boats serenely bobbing up and down. I heard you could put more than a hundred boats out there.

The harbor curved out of view further inland. I covered my eyes with my hand and I was able to shield enough glare to make out the faint line, in the distance, where the submarine net crossed the entire harbor, separating it from the open ocean.

We were coming in slightly from the west. This part of the harbor was taken up by the freight yards. Prince Rupert was built at the end of the railroad line, so tracks have always been its history, but over the past two years they'd multiplied like rabbits. There must have been twenty sets of tracks branching off the main line. Each line was filled with freight cars, all waiting to be unloaded and stored. The problem was that they could get them here a lot faster than they could unload them. To make matters worse, they were running out of places to store things. I'd heard at school they were thinking of using the school gym as storage. Nothing dangerous though, like explosives or weapons, although tons of those were in those freight cars.

Just over from the freight yards ran the dry dock. Two big ships sat in berths being repaired. They were American ships that had run aground coming through Telegraph Passage by the mouth of the Skeena.

Between fixing those ships, building new ones and doing general repair work, the shipyards were working seven days a week, twenty-four hours a day. They had almost two thousand people working there, not even counting the soldiers who guarded it and the big fuel storage yards off to the side.

The main streets of the town run straight, either parallel or on right angles to the harbor. It was strange to see traffic on the wide streets. Before the military got here, there were practically no cars or trucks. There wasn't much point since there was no place to go.

The road out of Rupert ran over to the mainland and then stopped about eight miles later. Now there were jeeps, big trucks carrying supplies, and those strange "ducks," trucks that could go into the water. Soldiers, sailors and even a few fliers were always on the street.

Most things in your life seem to get smaller as you get bigger. This hadn't happened to Prince Rupert. I got older and it got bigger. Before the war, Rupert was a sleepy little town of six thousand people. It had been that way for years and years. But in the last two years it had just exploded. The sign saying Welcome to Prince Rupert, listed the population. It seemed like they should have a little man with a paint brush just standing there changing it by the minute. Now it read Population 21,000.

We left the sidewalk to move around a sandbag barrier built to provide protection for an anti-aircraft gun. "Wow," I said, looking up at the gun barrel.

We stopped right in front of it and stared. The two guards, carrying rifles and wearing helmets stood silently over to our side, by the entrance to the bunker.

"Pretty amazing," Tadashi said. "There are six of them scattered around town. I was here with my father a couple of weeks ago, during the evening, and they had an air raid alert."

"Just a practice, right?"

"Yeah, but they sure acted like it was real. All the blackout screens were pulled down, lights turned out, people scrambling into their trenches, soldiers running around, the guns all got ready to fire."

"Must have been exciting."

"Yeah, it was. As long as it's all just pretend it's pretty exciting."

"It makes you wonder, though," I said.

"About what?"

"Well, except for Mr. and Mrs. Schultz and their daughter, I don't think there's a German within two thousand miles of here."

"Germans? It's not the Germans they're getting ready for," Tadashi said.

"Well, who's it for, then?"

"Come on, Jed, don't play dumb. You know as well as me, it's for the Japanese."

"I hear rumors but they're just rumors," I shrugged. "We're not at war with Japan. Why would we fight the Japanese?"

"Don't you ever listen to the radio?"

"You know we don't have one."

"I thought maybe at one of the other houses. You know, one of your relatives in the village."

"I don't think anybody has a radio."

"How about the papers?"

"Sometimes we get the *Daily News*. I usually read only the sports page and the funnies."

"You better start reading the rest. Things are happening in Japan. Not good things."

"I heard a little about it. They're fighting over there, right?"

"They're at war with China, and have taken over parts of Korea," he answered somberly. "There's talk about how Japan is building up its armies, and making more and more ships and planes. Some of the people in my village, people born in Japan, are following what's going on pretty closely."

"I guess they're just interested like I'm always wanting to know what's happening in Europe 'cause my father's there."

"That's part of it. But some of them, not many but a few, think it's just great. Japan, the rising sun, sweeping over Asia." He shook his head slowly. "The way they talk, it sounds like they're discussing a baseball game, not people killing each other."

I opened my mouth to answer when a shout interrupted.

"All right you two, move along!" yelled one of the soldiers. He'd left the entrance and moved in our direction. I turned around to see who he was yelling at and saw there was nobody there.

"Go on, beat it!" he yelled as he stopped right on top of us. "You, kid, get out of here and take the little Jap with you. We don't allow no fish-head nips to be spying on our installations."

I stumbled forward, away, and then stopped when I realized Tadashi hadn't moved. He was standing stock still.

"Tadashi, come on!" I called, but he didn't respond.

"Move it, Jap, or I'll make you move," the soldier threatened.

I rushed back and grabbed Tadashi by the arm. He turned his head towards me and the look of rage on his face was so intense that for an instant I hardly recognized him. Shocked, I loosened my grip.

The soldier pushed his body right up against Tadashi, and the only thing separating them was the rifle he was holding with both hands across his chest. "Get moving, ya little fish-head!" he yelled and then pushed the barrel of the gun against Tadashi's chest, knocking him backwards.

Tadashi staggered, regained his balance and then stepped forward a bit. I stared in disbelief. What was he doing? Tad never even argued with anyone and here he was having a shoving match with some guy with a gun.

I grabbed Tadashi from behind, struggled to pull him back a few steps and then slid around to the front so I was standing between him and the soldier.

"Better go along with your friend, nip!"

"Come on Tadashi, come on …" I pleaded, looking him squarely in the face.

"Get out of here, now, while I still let you," the soldier threatened.

"It's not worth it," I said quietly, "come on."

He nodded his head in agreement and the look of fire faded from his eyes. He stopped struggling against me and I released my grip.

"First smart thing you're done. Now just go running off with your little injun friend. Even an injun's got enough smarts not to mess with me," he taunted.

I felt the hair on the back of my neck bristle. What did he mean injun? Who was he calling an injun? I turned around and took a step towards him.

"Private Fletcher!" came a voice from the gun placement.

The soldier spun around. My eyes caught a movement at the entrance of the gun installation and I saw another soldier coming. He was older, maybe my father's age. He came to a stop right in front of us. He was an officer.

"Private Fletcher, return to your post," he ordered. His voice was stern and forceful.

"Yes, sir," the soldier said and marched away.

After he was out of earshot, the officer spoke. "Are you boys okay?"

I nodded. Tadashi didn't respond.

"I apologize. Most of these men are young and some are a little jumpy. They've listened to too many stories about the Japanese coming. Are you Japanese?" he asked.

"No," Tadashi replied.

"Well, why didn't you just tell him you were Chinese and he would have left you alone? The Chinese are okay. Most of us can't tell one of you from the other," he added, trying to sound friendly.

"I'm not Chinese," Tadashi replied.

"Not Chinese and not Japanese. What are you?"

"Canadian," Tadashi answered and then walked away.

.3.

"Mom! Naani! I'm home!" I bellowed as I pushed in through the front door. The screen slammed shut behind me, acting as a noisy punctuation mark for my entrance.

"You's yelling too loud to get my attention," Naani said as she came out of the kitchen, "and not nearly loud enough if you want your mother to hear you."

"She isn't here? Where is she?"

"The camp. Couldn't come home. The other cook just up and quit so she has to stay until they can get somebody else. A soldier come over, banging on all the houses 'til he found me." She paused. "You look like your dog just got shot," she joked as she read the disappointment in my face.

"Maybe this'll cheer you up," she said as she pulled a letter out of her apron pocket. "Joe just delivered it. It's from your father."

"AAAHHH!" I screamed. I slumped into the old weathered couch by the door.

"What's wrong? I thought this would make you happy."

"Don't you remember? Mom and me made a deal we'd only open Dad's letters when we were together."

She nodded her head sympathetically. "Too bad. Mmmmm ... maybe if the fish won't go to the net you have to bring the net to the fish."

Instantly I knew what she meant. "Could I?"

"Stay for dinner. Then go up to the camp. Circle around to the far side by the kitchen, come in real quiet and nobody will know nothin."

"What if I get caught? That major doesn't like me there."

"Well, that's easy," she said with a big smile on her face. "Don't get caught."

"That's not so easy."

"Don't go then."

"But I want to open the letter, I want to see Mom."

"Then go. What's the worst that can happen? They aren't gonna shoot ya."

I nodded my head.

"Come, take a bite to eat and I'll pack you a part to take to your momma. Everything they eat there comes out of cans so she'll be happy to see you with that letter, but even happier if ya bring her dinner. Now, you go and get your knapsack, game bag and rifle, and I'll go and put out your food."

"My rifle?"

"Well, you never know when you might come across some game," she answered slyly, as she moved out of the room.

I followed her. "Come on, Naani, there's no way any game will be anywhere near the camp. Any animal that hangs around all that commotion is too stupid to kill. Why do you really want me to take my gun?" I asked, although I already knew the answer.

"Just in case, you know, just in case. Animals … creatures … spirits …" she said, letting the sentence trail off without an ending.

"Naani," I scolded her. "First off, I'm not going deep into the forest. Second, I don't believe in all that forest spirit stuff, and, third, what makes you think a gun could hurt spirits, anyway?"

"Don't argue with me. I didn't get this old without getting wise. Just listen to me."

"Okay, I'll take my gun, but if I shoot any spirits, you have to clean and cook em," I answered as I swung my arms around her wrinkled old neck.

The Tsimshian, the old time Tsimshian, like my grandmother, live their whole lives right where the forest meets the sea. They never venture too far into the forest or too far out on the ocean. They believe both are inhabited by spirit creatures which take on the form of animals. These creatures are mostly good and playful, but if provoked or shown disrespect, they can be malicious or even deadly. Of course, I don't believe in that stuff.

Still, I was glad to take my rifle along. The sun would be setting before I got back and I do believe in things like cougars and bears and badgers. The mountains are full of animals. Most of the time they turn and run when they hear people coming, but you just can't predict everything an animal will do. If it was up to me, and my mother says it isn't, I'd bring my gun everywhere, including bed. Carrying a gun around was one of the few advantages of being up here. People would go crazy if I wandered around Victoria with my rifle.

Within fifteen minutes I chowed down and was on my way. The camp was about three miles as the eagle flew. Of course, I couldn't hope to follow any sort of straight path. I'd have to detour around rocky outcrops, deep bogs, impenetrable underbrush and fallen trees. The last time Mom was home she mentioned they'd started to send out sentries to guard the outside of the camp. When I got close I'd swing wide to avoid the guards and come at it from the far side.

Finding the camp would have been easy even if I didn't know the forest. The sounds of the bulldozers and chain saws echoed through the trees for miles. And even if you were deaf, the smell of those machines was just as easy to follow. I figured it was the smell of gas, even more than the sounds, which had driven the animals away.

The camp started as a thin line of brown dirt snaking its way through the jungle of green. When people think of jungles, they always think of Africa or South America or some other tropical place. But with all the rain we get here the forest is just like a jungle. I've seen how quickly it can swallow up an old path or an abandoned house.

The road reached up into a spot in the forest high enough to allow both a view of the harbor and a place to build a radio tower. At first this was just a brown patch at the end of the road. Day by day, bulldozer by chain saw, it grew bigger and bigger. The underbrush was stripped away and the solid green canopy, sometimes hundreds of feet above the ground, was cut down.

People who've never seen a Douglas fir just don't know how gigantic they can be. Everybody knows trees get big, but big doesn't even start to describe them. Some of them are so huge you could cut a hole in the middle large enough to drive a car right through. The tops of the tallest trees look like they reach right up to the sky. In fact, some of them are over two hundred feet tall.

As big as they are standing, it's frightening to watch one of them coming down. I saw them cut one of the big ones down at the camp. The sound was like a freight train steaming through the night. Even though I wasn't standing anywhere near it, I felt a surge of air rushing out of the way, and then, unbelievably, I felt the ground jump up.

Those soldiers, most of them from back east — none of them with any experience taking down trees — had no idea. The army tried to keep everything that happened really hush-hush, but in a place as small as Prince Rupert, there were no secrets. Especially if your mother worked there. The first few trees they felled came down in ways and directions that weren't expected. Bulldozers, jeeps, and buildings were smashed. These at least could be replaced. But there were tragedies as well. People got hurt and one man was killed. I heard the tree fell squarely on top of him and he was driven straight down into the ground like a tent peg. My mother told me they had to dig him up to bury him again. At first they used dynamite, tons of it, to try to blast away the rocks, as well as the tree stumps after they had cut down the trees. They got better with experience. And smarter. You just couldn't make a base here like you could down south. You had to build around things, not just over top of them. Finally they learned to leave the really big trees and rocks and built around them.

The camp came up on me sooner than I expected. The bulldozers and chain saws had become quiet a few minutes before. I was amazed at how much bigger it had got since my last visit three weeks ago. At the very center, where they had started, all the trees had been taken down. The sky was exposed and the ground was a sea of brown mud. Toward the outside, the big trees still stood but the underbrush and smaller trees had been cleared away.

Breaking up the brown of the earth were the buildings littering the ground. They'd started trying to lay the buildings out in a proper military style; straight lines with regular spaces between the buildings. Pretty soon they had the sense to give it up and the layout of the base now had more in common with our village than any plan they started with. I counted fifteen buildings. That was five more than the last time. This was a problem. The mess, which was where my mother slept in a bedroom off the back, was no longer at the edge of the clearing, backing into the trees. Now the cover of the forest was at least twenty-five yards away and I'd have to pass almost directly under the windows of more than one building to get there.

A wooden boardwalk ran between all the buildings. At places it was elevated far off the ground with steps leading up and down. They needed the boardwalk because the ground, exposed to rain every day and without any plants to absorb or hold it, had turned into a sea of churning mud. The only places where there wasn't mud was where there was rock. The gravel paths they'd put down before the boardwalk just kept on disappearing into the mud as the men walked on them.

At the center of the camp was a large, flat piece of rock. This open space, about the size of a baseball infield, was the parade grounds. The mess, officer's club, showers and commander's office all bordered this area. In the middle of the grounds a flag pole flew the Union Jack which flapped at the top.

One other change I noticed was a series of targets which had been placed along the east side of the camp. Directly behind them, forming a high wall, lay the newly killed corpse of a giant Douglas fir. I figured this was a practice shooting range, and the tree was meant to capture any stray bullets which missed the targets. I'd watched them taking target practice before. I couldn't believe how bad some of them were. I only hoped the Germans were even worse.

From my hiding spot, beneath the skirt of an evergreen tree which reached right to the ground, I scanned the camp. There were only a few men in sight, heavy boots sounding against the wooden walkways. They were moving toward the mess hall. Glancing at my father's watch which he gave me when he left, I saw it was a few minutes after five o'clock. I knew almost everybody on base was now inside the mess, having supper. Most of the men would be eating and then getting ready for leave down in Rupert. I heard a few voices, loud laughter and then the slamming of a screen door. Two soldiers had come out of the building just off to my left and strolled away.

The sweet smell of a fire found its way to my nostrils. Over to the right, a good hundred yards away, there was a blaze burning in the fire pit. A thick pall of smoke rose straight up, until it got to just above the level of the tallest trees, and then it was caught by wind and blown away. Ever since they'd started clearing away the space for the camp there'd been a fire burning, night and day, getting rid of all the scrub and wood. Tadashi's father had told me that on a clear day you could see the smoke rising up over the camp from way out on the water. The fishing boats could use it like a beacon to find their way back to port.

I sat down against the trunk of the tree. The fallen pine needles formed a cushion between me and the ground. To get to my mother, I'd have to move across camp, over open territory, directly to the back door of a building that held almost every soldier at the base. I dug a hand deep into my pocket and pulled out the letter. I thought about what my Naani had said; Easy, just don't get caught. I had to give it a chance.

"Move it! Come on outa there!" a voice screamed.

My heart almost jumped out of my throat. Who was it? Were they yelling at me?

"Get out! Shoo!" screamed a second voice, this one much deeper than the first.

I held my breath. Maybe they …

Baanngg! The sound was deafening, instantly accompanied by the whizzing of a bullet past my ear and the twang of a branch snapping.

I threw myself against the ground and sharp pine needles imbedded themselves in my hands and face. I heard yelling in the distance, and the sound of doors slamming and heavy feet against the wooden walkways. I heard voices from all sides of the tree. Out through the thick branches I saw pairs of feet and legs, a safe distance back from the tree. Lying perfectly still, I suspected I was invisible unless I moved.

"Everyone quiet!" a voice called out in an English accent like my father's.

There was silence. Then I heard the voice, and one or two others, but I couldn't make out the words. Silence, and then that voice came again, calm and quiet.

"If there is a person beneath the tree, you should come out at once. If you do not, we will assume it is some sort of animal and will commence firing."

On all fours I crawled, branches whacking me in the face. I cleared the last branch, my left arm gave way and I crashed face forward into the thick mud. Lifting my head, I tried to brush the mud away from my eyes with my mud-covered hands. I looked up to find myself in the middle of dozens of soldiers, all with their rifles trained on me. I opened my mouth to speak but no words came out.

"Put your weapons down," came the voice, which I now realized belonged to Major Brown. He stood directly in front of me.

I'd never had a gun, loaded or unloaded, pointed at me; I felt a rush of relief as the rifles were lowered.

"So, this is what a mountain lion looks like," Major Brown said sarcastically to one of the soldiers at his side. "Bring him to my office." He turned and walked away. He stopped ten paces away and turned around again.

"And send me the sentries who are on guard. I want them to explain how he managed to get by them."

Two pairs of arms grabbed me and I was pulled up, and off the ground, to be set back down on my feet on the walkway.

"Mighty stupid. Coulda got yourself shot," said one of the soldiers.

"After the major gets through with you, you might wish you had been shot," chuckled the other.

"Could somebody go back and get my gun?" I croaked.

"Your gun?"

"My rifle. I dropped it under the tree."

"Private!" he yelled over his shoulder to one of the soldiers who was walking behind us. "Go back to the tree and find the kid's weapon."

We moved along the walkway, crossed the table rock of the parade grounds, past the flagpole, the rope twanging against the metal pole, and came right to the major's office. The officer knocked.

"Come," came the reply through the closed door.

One soldier opened the door while the other pushed me forward so I entered before them.

"Here he is, sir, the prisoner, sir."

"Prisoner?" Major Brown questioned.

"Yes, sir," the soldier said very formally. "Do you wish us to stay sir, to act as guards, sir?"

"I think I shall be safe. Sit," he ordered, fixing me with a steely gaze.

I heard the door close. The two soldiers had beaten a hasty retreat.

"Explain your presence on my base."

"I was just coming to visit my mother," I stammered. I found it impossible to meet his gaze and looked down at my muddy feet. "I wanted to give her this letter from my father," I added, pulling it from my pocket. It too was mud stained.

"Your mother?"

"Naomi … Mrs. Blackburn."

"I thought you looked familiar, hard to tell through all that mud on your face. We've met on one of your too-frequent visits here."

"Yes, I mean … yes, sir."

"Why didn't you come in through the front gate?"

"I took the short-cut," I lied.

He nodded his head in agreement, but he looked like he didn't believe a word I'd said.

"Sergeant!" he barked, and I jumped slightly out of my seat.

The door opened instantly and a soldier appeared at my side.

"Bring Mrs. Blackburn."

"Yes, sir." The soldier turned on his heels and hurried out the door.

It would be good to have my mother here to protect me from this man. Then I thought, who would protect me from my mother? There was a knock on the door.

"Come."

The door opened, but instead of my mother, it was a soldier carrying my rifle and backpack.

"What are those?" the major asked the soldier.

"His," he said, motioning to me. "Found … under the tree, sir."

"Put them on the desk and leave, private."

The soldier responded quickly and was gone. I noticed that he, like the other soldiers, seemed fearful of the major.

"Why did you need a rifle to deliver a letter?"

"For protection or to hunt," I answered. I thought it best not to mention to fend off the spirits.

"Do you hunt?"

"Yes, most days."

"With success?"

"Most times," I said. This time I tried hard to keep my eyes focused on his but failed and my gaze again fell to the floor.

"My men have had less success. So far all they've got

are mosquito bites, sprained ankles, and lost."

"Not much game, close in here."

"No, nothing. That is why I did not believe it when the sentry said he had taken a shot at a mountain lion under a tree. A wild animal is too clever to be seen by any of this lot. What were you doing under the tree?"

"Just watching," I again lied.

"Watching? Were you hoping to see something funny?"

"Funny? I don't understand."

"You are not alone. Watching these, shall we say soldiers, in training, is at best amusing. Thank goodness the nearest German soldier is over six thousand miles away. Then, again, it isn't the Germans we're here to worry about. Where is your father that he needs to write you letters?"

"He's in England," I answered. "He's a fighter pilot. Spitfires," I answered. This time my eyes remained locked on his. I saw a look of acknowledgment

"Main event. That is where the war is happening. The place where they should put soldiers with experience, not in some summer camp thousands of miles away. I envy your father. Your mother never mentioned any of this."

"She doesn't like to talk about it."

"You should be very proud of him."

"I am."

He looked down at his wrist watch. "Now, if your mother would only honor us with her presence." His voice had softened.

The door flung open without a knock, and my mother ran in. She came directly to me and gave me a big hug.

"Are you all right?"

"Yes, I'm fine." I felt embarrassed to be hugged in front of the major.

She turned to him. "You better explain yourself. How

dare your men fire at my son!" Unlike the soldiers she had no fear of him. I'd never known her to be afraid of anybody.

"Firstly, Mrs. Blackburn, it was an accident, and secondly, as you would know if you knew my men, the safest place to be when they shoot is where they are aiming. Believe me, that man will be dealt with. Now, would you please pull up a chair and join us?"

She crossed over to his desk and picked up my gun and knapsack. She placed the rifle in my hands and put the knapsack on her lap as she sat down.

"Your son says he is here to deliver a letter to you. I will forgive him for trespassing on a military base, out of respect for you and your husband, but I do not believe that is all there is to his visit."

I again found my eyes focusing on the floorboards.

"Of course, there's more to it," my mother answered.

I looked at her in shock. What more could there be?

"He brought something for you," she said, patting the knapsack.

What was she talking about, I thought as she started to unbuckle the bag.

"Here, I'll have to warm it up, but you can tell from the smell even when it's cold, how wonderful it'll taste." She pulled out the container holding the cooked rabbit and placed it on his desk.

The major took off the layer of wrapping and peered inside. He closed his eyes and inhaled deeply. A sigh escaped his lips.

"I thought you and the officers might be tired of all the canned food I have to keep giving you," my mother said.

"Tired does not cover it, Mrs. Blackburn. As a soldier I always thought the lead I needed to fear was from a bullet and not from the canned food I was forced to eat."

"I heard you and your supply officer talking about

how much it costs to get food up here and I got to thinking that maybe we could get better food, cheaper, from right around here. Not enough for everybody, all the time, but maybe at least something different every now and again."

"I've had the same idea but we've had no success," he said shaking his head. "My men have only been able to catch a cold. All these men with guns and the closest they come to shooting anything is your son."

"I'm not talking about the soldiers, Major, I'm talking about my son."

"Your son!"

"Yep. Best little hunter around here. Nobody can hunt like a Tsimshian and he's half Tsimshian."

I hardly ever thought of myself as Native.

She continued. "Pay him the same price per pound you pay for the canned food for any game he brings in. If he doesn't get anything you don't have to pay him anything."

"Sounds reasonable," the major replied.

"Plus all the ammunition he uses, a soldier's jacket so he isn't mistaken for a mountain lion again, he gets to keep the skins, and," she paused, " twenty-five cents per hour to help me around the kitchen. I need some help around here."

"I don't think that I can …"

My mother leaped to her feet and pulled the rabbit stew out from underneath his nose.

"In that case, if you have no hunter, you have no special meals, no sample snack tonight and maybe no cook tomorrow."

The major fixed her with a steely gaze. She stared right back. They were locked together for a few seconds and then he looked down.

"As I was saying. I do not think I can have him accept less. Now, if you and your son leave so that you can prepare my meal, we shall sit down later and finalize things."

My mother smiled. "You will have yourself both a good meal, and a good deal."

She took me by the arm, a smile still on her face, and pulled me to my feet. I felt her nails dig into my skin right through my jacket. Her arm slipped around my waist and we walked out the door and along the walkway, now crowded with men.

"It's my son," she said a couple of times in explanation.

She led me off the boardwalk and around the side of the mess to her small quarters, behind the kitchen. She wasn't talking but I could see, out of the corner of my eye, that she still wore a smile. She pulled open the screen door and gestured for me to enter. Quietly, and with calm deliberation, she let the screen door close and then pushed closed the inner, solid door. She walked directly up to me and put her hands on both sides of my face. She squeezed. Hard.

"What do you think you're doing?" she said with quiet menace.

"I wath …" I stopped. With her hands tightly gripping my face there was no way I could answer.

"You almost got shot! You shouldn't have come up here!" She released my face and her arms slipped around my shoulders. I hugged her back.

"How did you know about the food from Naani?"

"Have you got a head cold? I could smell it as soon as I picked up the knapsack."

"Am I really going to be paid to hunt?"

"Of course. I'd been thinking about it for the past few days. The other cook quit because of all the complaints about the food. Can't turn canned crap into good food," she added, shaking her head in resignation. "Your Naani wouldn't believe how they eat."

"So you just put things together to come up with

that story? I never knew you were such a good liar."

She gently cuffed me on the side of the head. "Don't talk to your mother that way. Besides, now I'm more than your mother, I'm your boss. Now, where is that letter?"

I pulled it from my pocket once again.

"Wonderful!"

She took the envelope and ripped open the back, and pulled the letter from within.

"What does it say?" I asked urgently. "What does it say?"

"Come over here beside me, and we'll read it together," she replied. She sat down in a comfortable chair.

I came over and perched on the arm of the chair.

Dear Naomi and Jed,

I hope this letter finds you both well. I'm sure that between your work at the camp and Jed's at school you're both very busy. Hopefully, so busy that you don't miss me as much as I miss both of you.

Most of the time here I'm very bored. We sit around and play cards and shoot a little pool. The food isn't very good, but I guess you know that no army cook is any good (ha-ha). I get in my plane for a couple of hours every day or so. Mostly the same thing every time. Nothing too exciting or dangerous Almost every single time I flew my bush plane there was more danger, so don't worry about me.

Say hello to Naani for me as well as everybody else. I'm fine here so don't worry.

Love,
Dad

My mother folded the paper in two and looked up at me.

"Your father is a much better flyer than he is a liar."

"I know."

"He just doesn't want us to worry, is all."

"Easier said than done," I answered. "No matter what he says I'm going to worry."

"Me too," she said quietly, "me too."

.4.

The very best spot in the entire camp was right around the side of the mess hall, by the door to the kitchen. In the morning when there was a chill in the air — and that was every day now that October was more than half over — the sunlight bounced off the building and formed a big, bright puddle to warm my bones. Sitting right there, I hardly needed to even turn my head to see the parade grounds right in front of me, the road into town, the motor pool, the major's office, showers, officers' club, three of the barracks, and of course the mess itself. There wasn't much happening around here that didn't happen right in front of my face.

I'd been up here often since I'd been given the job two weeks before. My mother was still the only cook. They hadn't been able to find anybody else to do the job, which wasn't surprising. Everybody who wanted a job could get one at the cannery, or dry dock or the rail yards. There were lots of jobs going begging, jobs that paid more than an army cook. Mother said that as long as I was around she'd keep working, so I was here a few nights after school and most of the weekends. When I wasn't working, I was free to just wander around the base and check things out. There was always something to check out.

The base was coming along. The latest additions were the showers. They'd picked up an old boiler off a ship that had been scrapped at the Prince Rupert dry dock. They'd brought it up on the back of a flatbed truck, and then taken a bulldozer and dragged it into position. It held hundreds of gallons of water. They heated water for the showers by burning all the bush they'd taken down. If all the men were careful and took short showers, there was enough water for everybody. This was one of the only luxuries in the camp. After working all day in the mud and rain, covered with sap and sweat and sawdust, the men happily hit the showers. I'd seen tempers flare up a couple of times when people took too long in the shower and used up somebody else's water.

"Are you going to peel that thing or make a pet of it?" my mother asked.

I was lost in thought and her voice startled me. I dropped the potato.

"That's no way to treat a pet," she chided me.

I bent over and picked it up. "How long have you been standing there?"

"For a couple of potatoes. You were doing fine until you came to that last one."

From the door behind my mother one of the men, Smitty, came strolling out, munching on an apple.

"Hi, Mrs. Blackburn. Hi, Jed. Anything you need in town, ma'am?"

"No, I think we're okay, but thanks for asking."

Smitty's real name was John Smith and he was a sergeant who ran the motor pool. He was the only soldier my mother would let come into the kitchen or use the back door. He could wander through, help himself to things in the fridge, get a fresh coffee or even sit down at the small table and eat back there with us. Often he waited until everybody else had finished eating and then he, my mom and me would eat together.

Smitty was in his late twenties but looked younger. He had a mop of brown hair that seemed out of control despite the short military haircut. He said when it was going to rain his hair got frizzy. Since there was hardly a day in Rupert when it didn't rain, his hair was permanently frizzed. He was tall, and skinny, well over six feet, with large feet and hands. My mother joked she only let him in the kitchen because she was trying to fatten him up. I knew while she was kidding around, this was at least part way true. Despite the fact you hardly ever saw him without food in his mouth, he was as skinny as a rail.

Smitty had told me he'd joined the army when he was sixteen. He didn't have much family, and the family he had didn't think much of him. I found that was the big reason he hung around the kitchen. Although my mother really wasn't much older than Smitty, she was kind of a mother to him.

My mother was always careful about me being around the soldiers too much. She figured they might teach me things she didn't want me to know, or at least didn't want me to know quite yet. She trusted Smitty though and he'd taken me out on details.

"I wonder what's going on over there?" Smitty asked.

My mother and I spun around to see a crowd of men moving across the parade grounds.

"Looks like a circus," my mother answered.

"Better check it out. Jed, you want to come along? I mean if it's okay with your mom."

"Go ahead, you'll have plenty of time to peel potatoes before supper."

Smitty bounded down the stairs and towards the action. Smitty never walked when he could run. He was like a clock with its mainspring wound just a little too tight.

Already a good-sized crowd had gathered. We reached men at the back of the crowd. People were craning their necks and squirming to try to get a better view. There was also a group of men standing against the rail on an adjoining part of the elevated walkway, trying to see the goings on.

"I can't see a thing," I said.

Smitty tapped one of the men on the back. "What's happening? What's the story?"

"They got themselves a bird, a big bird. They're going to tie it up to the pole," he answered.

"A bird? What sort of bird would attract an audience like this?" I wondered.

"What are we talking about here, a big chicken or a turkey?" Smitty asked with a deadpan expression. Smitty hardly ever said anything seriously but always kept a straight face. Even though I knew what to expect, he still surprised me sometimes.

"Naw, don't be silly," the soldier responded, "it's one of those big eagles. A couple of the guys found it and brought it back."

"I want a closer look at this," Smitty answered.

"Don't get yourself too close, though," the soldier cautioned. "One of the guys who found the bird is getting stitched up now. Bird took a good swipe out of his side."

"Thanks for the advice. What time is it, Jed?"

I looked at my watch. "About ten minutes to one."

"Good," said Smitty. "As soon as the whistle sounds at one o'clock, most of these guys have to go back to their work details. You and I can get a real up close look then. Let's grab a bite while we're waiting."

I didn't want to leave, but looking at the wall of men standing between us and the eagle, I nodded in agreement. We circled around to the side of the mess and went in through the back door. My mother had just come back through the swinging doors carrying a tray filled with dirty dishes.

"You were right, Mrs. Blackburn," Smitty nodded. "It is a circus and they've started collecting animals. They got themselves an eagle."

"It's always a circus around here," she answered. "I was talking to a couple of men who saw the bird being brought in. They told me a couple of the sentries found it on the edge of the camp, hiding in some underbrush."

Smitty took the tray from her hands, set it down and started scraping plates into the garbage can sitting by the sink. After clearing each plate he set it down in the soapy water.

"I wonder what happened to it?" I asked.

"Been shot probably," she muttered, shaking her head. "Just like dozens of them have been shot. Give a bunch of men guns and ammunition, and sure as night follows day they're going to start shooting at things." She started washing the dishes and I picked up a cloth to dry them.

"Is it badly hurt?" Smitty asked.

"Not sure. Heard them talking. They said it looks like one of the wings is broken, and that it's pretty weak. Probably hasn't eaten for a while."

"At least it's still alive," I offered.

"For now," she said quietly. "Probably be better off if it were dead."

Just as I was going to ask her what she meant, I heard the whistle go off to signal the end of the lunch break.

"I can't believe all the fuss. Grown men crowding around that poor bird like it's one of the wonders of the world. Some of them didn't even finish eating, didn't want to miss any of the excitement."

Smitty and I both stopped working and looked at each other. We wanted to go right now and check out the eagle. My mother stopped working as well and looked first at me and then at Smitty. It was always a little spooky how she could figure out what was going on in my head. Smitty had noticed that before, and said I should consider myself lucky, because his parents never knew what he was thinking about, even when he told them.

She shook her head. "Okay … fine … what difference will two more fools make?"

I balled up my cloth and tossed it on the counter.

"I'll try and keep a little something warm," she yelled as we rushed out the screen door.

Men were on the move and there were only half a dozen guys forming a loose circle, a large hole in the center, holding the eagle. Between the legs of the shuffling men I caught my first glimpse of the bird. We moved closer and people shifted to the side to allow us a spot.

The eagle stood at the side of the flagpole. It was a full grown bird, brown feathers except for the white atop its "bald" head. The white was streaked with a line of red. Dried blood. It looked like a bullet had creased it. One wing was held in tight to its body while the other, the left wing, was slightly extended and hung to the side. Its beak was part way open and it was panting, its chest visibly rising and falling. It moved its head from side to side, on a slight angle, in quick little jerking motions, like it was trying to see all the things going on around it. It had a look of pure rage and I involuntarily took a small step backwards as we locked eyes. The eyes were a pale shade of yellow, black pupils staring out from the very center. A piece of thick black leather was tied to one of the bird's legs, and attached to a rope which bound it to the pole. It was hard to tell how long the line was, but judging from the space between the eagle and the nearest soldier, I figured it was a little less than three feet.

During the whole time I'd lived or vacationed up here, I'd only ever seen eagles from a distance, usually way above my head. Along the Skeena River, especially when the salmon are running, the eagles are everywhere. They swoop down over the water and grab gigantic fish from the shallows, or eat the dead ones off the rocks. An eagle, with its wings outstretched farther than a man can reach, a salmon in its talons, would drop to the ground. Those powerful talons and beaks would rip the salmon to shreds and then in a flash it would be eaten. Along with the eagles, the big browns and grizzly bears wade into the shallows and line the shore like fat fishermen wearing ratty old fur coats. It always seems that even the bears give the eagles a wide passage.

When I was little, my parents had taken me to the Vancouver Zoo and we'd watched one in a cage. My mother had told me how important the eagle was to both the Tsimshian and Haida.

I hadn't paid much attention. I knew they were interesting and all, but that was it.

Later I realized half the stories my Naani told had an eagle in them, and the pictures and carvings and totems had eagles. To the Tsimshian, the eagle is more than a bird, it's part of their heritage, history and ancestry all rolled into one bundle of feathers.

"Wouldn't want to tangle with that thing," Smitty noted. "Bet those claws could tear you to pieces."

"Believe it," replied one of the soldiers. "Look at what it did to Washburn."

Washburn was standing off to the side. "Got me good," he said. I could see where his shirt was ripped. He pulled it up to reveal a patch of gauze, taped to his side, some blood staining through the cover.

"Are you one of the men who brought it in?" Smitty asked.

"Yeah, me and Watson and Ross."

"Where'd you find it?" I asked.

"Just north of the camp. It was hiding in a clump of cedars."

Smitty frowned. "How did you ever get it here, tied up?"

"It wasn't easy, believe me. One of the guys went back

for a tarp and we tossed it over top of the bird. It settled right down once we had its head covered."

"Why can't it fly?" I asked.

"Shot."

"Shot? You shot it?"

"No, not me. A couple of days ago, when I was on perimeter duty, I saw an eagle get shot down. Didn't see where it landed exactly, just heard the shot and saw it falling. I've been looking for it since then whenever I go on duty. Didn't think I'd find it, and really didn't think it would still be alive. I just thought I could take a few of its feathers when I found the carcass."

I wondered if this guy had been the one who had shot the bird. It was rumored the guards were taking pot shots at things, betting money on who could hit what. Targets were one thing but just shooting animals to see if you could do it was pretty lousy.

Smitty turned to me and spoke quietly. "Washburn wouldn't have shot it," he said, reading my mind. "He's a good guy." He turned back to Washburn. "What's going to happen to it?"

"Major Brown put in a call for the local vet to come and have a look at it. I didn't think old Brown had any soft spots, but it seems the major is an animal lover. Wants to see if somehow it can be fixed up."

Suddenly, without warning the eagle spread its wings and tried to leap up. It got slightly airborne and then crashed to the ground. All of us standing near it jumped away. One wing lay stretched out and bent.

It was ironic how I had wanted to get close to see the bird, and now, standing right in front of it, I wanted to get away. The creature seemed so sad sitting there in the mud, tethered to a pole.

"I'm going to go and help my mother."

"Not so fast, Jed. Go and ask her for some meat, raw meat. What do eagles eat?"

"Fish, small game like rabbits and groundhogs," I answered.

"Didn't you bag a bunny, yesterday?"

I nodded.

"Good. Ask your mother if she still has some of it around. Even if she's already cleaned the carcass, bring back the skin, head and paws."

I turned to follow his request.

"And Jed, hurry, there's no telling how long this bird has gone without food."

By the time I came back, carrying the hind quarters of the rabbit, Smitty was by himself, squatting in the dirt, watching the eagle.

"Where'd everybody go?" I asked.

"I put them all to work."

This didn't surprise me. Smitty was only a sergeant but people, even the officers, seemed to listen to him.

"I wanted the eagle to be more comfortable. I sent two guys to the workshop to build a lean-to, two more to get a large branch it could use for a perch, one guy to get fresh water and the rest out to cut up small cedars."

"What are the cedars for?"

"The bird looks scared. I thought if it had a place to hide, sort of like a blind, it would feel safer and calmer," he answered. "I don't know how hurt it is, but if it keeps leaping up in the air it's going to break its neck too."

"What do you want me to do with this?" I said, gesturing to the remains of the rabbit.

"Guess."

"Don't be such a wise guy. I meant, do you want me to give it to the bird now or wait?"

"Now's good."

I tossed the meat and it skittered across the ground, bumping into the eagle's feet. The bird jumped backwards.

"First time I've ever heard of an eagle being afraid of a rabbit," I chuckled.

"Especially a dead rabbit."

The eagle cocked its head to the side, tentatively reached out a talon to poke the rabbit, and then drew its leg back. This was repeated a second and then a third time. Finally, the eagle leapt into the air and landed squarely on the leg. The talons disappeared into the flesh as the eagle sat atop the carcass, and it let out a screech. The bird reached down and with its powerful curved beak tore a large strip off the carcass. It tossed the meat slightly into the air and then, in one big gulp, swallowed it down. It repeated this process, again and again.

A car, a brown Ford, pulled through the main gate. It came to a stop and a smallish man carrying a black bag got out.

"Are you the vet?" Smitty asked.

"Yes, I am. And I'd be a happier vet if I was going to examine a dog or cat."

"I guess people don't often bring their pet eagles to see you," Smitty deadpanned.

"Parrots and budgies, yes, eagles no."

"Same thing, pretty much, isn't it?" Smitty asked.

"One big difference. You never have to worry about a budgie biting off your finger or ripping you open."

"That is a difference," Smitty agreed. "How are you going to examine it?"

"Carefully. Very carefully and from a safe distance, at least at first."

The vet circled around the eagle and watched it rip apart the rabbit. Occasionally he'd nod his head or quietly mutter something.

"Is there any way you can get that meat away from it?" he asked Smitty.

"Sure, there's probably lots of ways. None of which I'm going to try."

The vet grimaced and nodded in agreement. "Could

we get it a mouse or a rat to eat?"

"That we could do," Smitty reassured him. Smitty turned to two of the men who had just brought back a large branch to use as a perch.

"Check out the mousetraps in the kitchen and barracks. If there are any mice, bring them back. Jed, go as well."

As the three of us headed off in different directions, I saw Major Brown come out of his office toward the eagle. I wanted to turn around and hear what was going to happen. Instead I started running. The faster I could get a mouse the faster I could come back.

The trap in the kitchen was empty. A second, in the corner of the mess, was equally deserted. Running out the front door, I almost knocked into three men walking to their work detail who were rubbernecking in the direction of the eagle. I sprinted along the walkway until I came to the officers' club. Opening the door, I pushed the magazine rack away from the wall. There it was! A mouse trap containing a mouse. The lump of cheese was in its teeth, the metal bar across the back of its broken neck. Instant death. I grabbed the mouse, trap and all, and sprinted back to the flagpole.

By now Major Brown and the vet were deep in conversation. Smitty and a couple of the other guys were standing off to the side, just within ear shot. I showed Smitty the mouse. He nodded.

I put my mouth close to Smitty's ear and spoke quietly. "What's going on? What are they talking about?"

Smitty turned so his back was to the conversation and softly spoke to me. "Major wants to know if it can be fixed. If not, he's going to shoot it."

"And?"

"So far the vet can't tell. Here, give me the mouse and come along."

We walked over to the two men. "Excuse us, sir, but

we have the mouse the vet requested."

"Good, good!" the vet replied.

He took the mouse and removed it from the trap. He then bent down and opened up his brown bag. He took out a small bottle and unscrewed the top. Inside were pills, and he shook three out of the container and into his hands.

"To fully answer your question, Major, I need to examine the eagle, and the only way I can examine it is to knock it out."

"How do you propose to do that?" asked Major Brown.

"With this mouse. This is the 'sugar' to disguise the medicine."

He proceeded to open up the little mouse's mouth and shoved the three pills down its tiny throat.

"Anybody got any string?" the vet asked.

"I do," one of the men volunteered. "Right here in my pocket." He pulled out a small spool. "It's not very strong," he said as the vet took it from him.

The vet tied a knot around the front legs of the little rodent. He pulled it snug.

He looked at me. "I want you to drag this around, get the eagle's attention, but don't let him have it. Get him interested. Do you understand?"

"Sort of. I'm just not sure why the eagle would want this little mouse when it already has the rabbit," I commented as I took the line.

"Because the rabbit is dead and you're going to make the mouse seem alive."

Every human eye was trained on me but the eagle seemed totally occupied with the rabbit. I felt embarrassed. I dropped the mouse to the ground and started walking, dragging it behind me.

"Move it with a little more energy," the vet suggested. "Make it dance around."

I jerked it back and forth. The eagle looked up from its meal and watched as the mouse ran back and forth in front of it. I did a circle right around it. The eagle turned its head all the way as far as it could, and then spun it in the opposite direction, so it could see it on the other side. There was no question I had its complete attention.

"Now, bring it over here," the vet commanded.

I brought the mouse to the vet's feet. He bent down and undid the knot. He handed the mouse, all covered with dirt, back to me.

"Here, throw it."

I pulled back my arm to really heave it.

"No!" he yelled. "I want you to throw it to the eagle, not through the eagle."

I followed his directions and pitched the mouse in the direction of the bird. It bounced off its perch atop the tattered remains of the rabbit and pounced directly on top of the mouse. In one swift motion, almost so fast it was a blur, it took the mouse with its talons, tossed it into the air and swallowed it down in one lump without chewing.

"Just a little nibble for that big fella," Smitty remarked.

"Perfect," the vet announced. "It should be about twenty minutes before the pills take effect. It would be better if we left the bird alone. The calmer it is the faster things should work. Place the cedar branches around it to give the eagle a feeling of safety."

While I helped place the cover, the vet, accompanied by the major, went into the mess hall. They'd probably get a coffee or slice of pie. My stomach growled and I remembered I hadn't eaten. Smitty had the same idea and, as soon as the last branch was placed, we high-tailed it for the back door of the kitchen.

My mother had two meals, under overturned pie

plates, sitting on the table. She didn't say a word as we tore into our meals. Lunch may have just ended but she was already getting supper ready at the counter. There were two soldiers, doing a punishment duty, working away at the sink. Between bites, Smitty glanced anxiously at his watch.

Without warning, Smitty jumped up from the table. "The mail!" he yelped. "I forgot the mail. It's all still sitting in my jeep. I'll get killed if something happens to it." He ran for the door, still chewing his last mouthful of food.

"Was there a lot of mail today?" my mother questioned.

Smitty stopped and propped the door open with his foot.

"Yep. Lots of letters and even more parcels."

"Parcels? What sort of parcels?"

"They're all wrapped up tight but most have blankets or coats or special treats or bread."

"Bread? Why would anybody send bread? By the time it got here it would be all stale. They can get my fresh baked bread anytime."

"Beats me," he answered, although the way he looked away, it was obvious he knew more than he was saying.

My mother had a thoughtful look on her face. "I smell something here and it isn't the smell of baking bread."

"I don't smell anything," Smitty answered. "I must have a head cold from all the rain."

Smitty let the door close and ran off across the parade ground.

I managed to stuff in enough food to stop my stomach from grumbling. It's amazing how fast you can eat if you don't waste any time chewing. While my mother had her back to me I brought my plate over to the garbage can and scraped off the remaining food. Dropping the plate into the soapy sink water, I hurried away.

"I'll be back later to help," I offered as an excuse.

There were cedars piled around the flagpole and I couldn't see the eagle. I wanted to see but had enough sense not to crowd right in. If those pills weren't working, I could find the eagle a lot faster, and a lot closer, than I wanted. The branch, which had been brought for the bird to use as a perch, was still off to the side. I sat down on it. Nothing to do but wait.

Fortunately the wait wasn't too long. The vet and Major Brown came out from the mess hall. The major still carried a mug and took sips as they moved forward.

"Well, Jed, is he asleep?" Major Brown asked.

"Haven't seen him, and there aren't any sounds."

"That's a good sign," the vet announced. He dug into his bag again and produced a pair of heavy canvas gloves. "But, just in case, these might help."

The vet started pulling away clumps of cedar branches. With each one I expected the eagle to come hurtling towards him. There was still no movement.

"Poor fella," he said quietly, and motioned for us to come closer.

The eagle was lying on its side, eyes closed, not moving. I was afraid it was dead. Then I could make out the faint movement of the chest going up and down. He picked up the eagle and cradled it gently. It filled his arms.

"Could you go over by my bag … Jed, isn't it? … I left a small hood right there on the ground."

I brought it over. He carefully placed it on top of the eagle's head and, using his teeth, pulled the drawstring at the bottom to secure it in place.

"He's off in dream land," the vet said. "Now, with the hood in place, even if he does wake up, we'll still be able to control him. Could I get some help?"

"Certainly, what do you need?" Major Brown asked.

"Just somebody to hold him while I perform the examination."

"I'll get somebody right away."

"What about this young man? He's been here from the start."

"Jed? Would that be all right with you?"

"Yeah ... I guess so," I replied cautiously.

The vet nodded. "Good. You aren't going to get too many chances in your life to hold an eagle. Come over here and take him in your arms."

I stepped forward, held out my arms and braced myself to take on the weight of the bird. Carefully, he placed the eagle with its hooded head toward mine.

"It's as light as a feather!" I noted in amazement. "It must be practically starving to death."

"No, he's not in bad shape. People are always surprised at how little an eagle, or any bird, really weighs. A full grown eagle weighs between ten and twelve pounds. They have to be built light to fly. Only land birds like ostriches or sea birds like penguins are heavy."

He started running his fingers through the bird's feathers, over the length of its body, working his way from the talons up to the head. I thought it would be pretty interesting to be a vet.

"No obvious injuries ... good muscle tone ... no abscesses ... hello, what do we have here?" His fingers probed the side of the head where the feathers were stained. "A small crease in the skull. No point of entry. Undoubtedly a very close shave from a bullet that just skipped off the side of the head. Major, can you come here?"

The major came over and stood directly in front of the vet. "Could you please take the wing after I stretch it out?"

He proceeded to pull the injured wing out. It extended at least three feet, maybe more. This bird, which stood almost three feet from talon to beak, was probably almost seven feet from the tip of one wing to the tip of the other. The vet placed one of his hands at what I figured was sort of the bird's elbow and his second hand went to the tip. He then felt his way along the length of the limb, carefully exploring.

Holding the eagle was like having a pillow in my hands. The soft feathers lightly moved with each shallow breath it took. I eased off my bottom hand and felt one of the talons pricking my skin.

"Well, I can't detect any obvious break," the vet said. "If the wing had been broken we would have had to put it to sleep."

I felt a surge of relief flood over me. I didn't want them to kill it.

"But, why can't it fly?" I asked.

"I suspect it has a torn muscle, probably sustained in the fall after the bullet grazed its head, knocking it out of flight. As well, although it's hard to tell how much of a factor this is, it does seem to be missing a number of prime wing feathers on the injured wing, which would make flight difficult."

"What will be the treatment?" Major Brown asked.

"We have to wait."

"For what?"

"To see what happens. If it's just feathers and a torn muscle, then time will allow both to repair and it should be able to fly again."

"Excellent," Major Brown replied.

"Until then, you'll have to keep it fed, watered and safe from further injury."

"We'll try. I have somebody in mind who might be able to take good care of it," Major Brown said, looking at me. "Somebody who'll take very good care of it … right, Jed?"

"Come on, if we move fast we can stay ahead of my sisters," Tadashi said as he came up to me on the path. I
fell in beside him and took up his pace.

"It will be different walking through the woods without your sisters giggling at our heels," I commented.

"Yeah, they can be such little pests. And it's always
worse when you're around."

"You're blaming me?"

"Not you, but Midori. It wouldn't be so bad if she
hadn't taken such a shine to you."

"A shine!"

"Yeah, she thinks you're real dreamy. Can't you tell
how she's always giving you cow eyes and laughing at
your jokes?"

"Everybody laughs at my jokes. I'm a funny guy."

"Not that funny, and not everybody," Tadashi responded.

"Well, everybody except Toshio." Toshio and another
kid from Sikima were walking up ahead of us. Like always he was talking too loud. I'd rather walk with
Tadashi's sisters then be around him. He and his family
had only just moved to the village this past summer and
he'd taken an instant dislike to me. His English was
getting better, but even in the beginning, when he
couldn't do much more than grunt, he made it pretty
clear he wanted to fight me. He was two years older

than me, but I was a full head taller and outweighed him.

"Toshio might think you're funny too, but he's too busy being jealous of all the attention Midori shows you."

"Jealous? Of me and Midori? She's just a kid. What is she, eleven years old?"

"She'll soon be twelve," Tadashi replied as he picked up a stick from the ground.

"Eleven, twelve, big difference."

"It is to Toshio. I think he'd like to make Midori his bride some day."

I could see what old Toshio might be thinking. I wouldn't admit it to anybody, heck.

I hardly admitted it to myself, but I could see where he could take a shine to Midori. She had big brown eyes, soft round features and was really pretty. She also had a sense of humor. But, she was years younger. I had my eye on a couple of girls at school. Girls my age. At least now it all made sense why this guy didn't like me.

"Come on, let's speed up and I'll give Toshio my blessing. Heck, I'll even get them a wedding present. Maybe then he'll go easy on me."

"It's my father's blessing he'll be asking. But he probably still won't feel any different towards you," Tadashi said.

"What else? Is he jealous of our friendship? Tell him he can marry you too," I joked.

"Other reasons," he replied quietly and I knew there was more beneath his somber expression.

"What other reasons?"

"You gotta understand, Jed, these Japanese can be a little strange."

"These Japanese? What do you mean 'these Japanese?' What do you think you are, an Eskimo?"

"You know what I mean. The *Issei*."

Issei are the people who were born in Japan. Mostly

those were just the older people, like parents and grand-parents. Almost all of them were now naturalized Canadian citizens. Those born in Canada, like Tadi and most of the other kids, are the *Nisei*.

"What sort of strange ideas?" I asked.

"I don't really want to talk about it."

"Then you shouldn't have started what you don't want to finish. Explain it to me."

"They just don't think a Japanese should marry somebody other than another Japanese."

"Yeah, well I think we both have it figured out I'm not planning on marrying your little sister."

"But it's more than that. They don't think that anybody should ever … look I told you I don't want to talk about this any more."

"Sounds like you don't know what you're talking about."

"Yeah, I know what I'm talking about. You can't get me to tell you by giving me a hard time. I'm not stupid you know. I'm no Toshio."

"Okay, okay," I admitted. "Although someday you may have a bunch of half-Toshio little nieces and nephews running around being confused."

Tadashi laughed. I liked to hear him laugh almost as much as he liked laughing. Tadi seemed to be almost always happy. Even when he was acting serious, I could usually catch a hint of laughter in his dark eyes. He was shorter and thinner than me, most of the Japanese were, but he was already bigger than his father. It was funny, but the kids born in this country usually became bigger than their parents, and if Toshio was any indication, bigger than those kids still being born in Japan.

"So, are you going to tell me?" I asked.

Tadashi gave a big sigh and slowly nodded his head. "Look, Jed. I want you to understand this isn't me or my family but some of the older, real Japanese. You know, the *Issei.*"

"Okay, I get the message, go on," I said, suddenly apprehensive.

"They figure everybody should stay in their own race. Not just the Japanese, but everybody. Japanese should marry Japanese. Chinese should marry Chinese. Whites should marry whites …"

"And Indians should marry Indians," I said, completing his sentence.

"Yeah," he confirmed, looking down at his shoes.

"So, they just don't understand about people like me, half white and half Indian."

"Yeah," he agreed, still looking down.

I'd been in lots of fights during my life over being called a "half-breed." It seemed like there was some yahoo in everyplace I ever lived. Funny thing was, I didn't even think of myself as part Indian. It wasn't like I didn't know my mother was native, but I thought of myself as being like my father.

"Well, anytime Toshio wants to have a run at me, I'll be ready for him. I'm a lot bigger than he is," I said, motioning up ahead at him. "Look at the little shrimp."

"Bigger doesn't matter if he knows judo."

"What's that?"

"It's a form of self-defense that uses holds and throws. Lots of schools in Japan teach it to the students."

"I'll teach him a few things if he tries anything with me," I said. "Like how far he can fly." I laughed.

"It's no joking thing, Jed. Judo uses leverage and it's better to be smaller than the guy you're fighting."

"Sounds pretty stupid to me. I always figured it was better to be bigger … a lot bigger." I started to laugh again.

"What's so funny?" Tadashi asked.

"Some ways it's good to know that Japanese can be as stupid as anybody else."

"Everybody's got their share of stupid. You just have to look at Toshio to know that. I gotta talk to my father, though. I can't bear the thought of half-stupid, half-Toshio nieces and nephews."

I laughed but there was one more question I needed to ask. "What about you?"

"What about me, what?"

"You've told me how Toshio would feel and how the old Japanese would feel, but how would you feel about me marrying your sister?"

"You and my sister? No way. Not a chance."

"Why not? You don't think I'm good enough because I'm a half-breed?"

"Well," Tadashi shrugged, "Jed, old friend, you're a half-breed who's half right. I actually don't think one of you is good enough for the other. You can do better than my bratty little sister, that's all."

"Better?"

"Yeah, better. If you're going to risk getting the Japanese mad at you, aim for the moon. Go after Kiyoka Azuma."

"Kiyoka!" She was almost eighteen, beautiful and engaged to be married. "Are you crazy?" I snorted.

"My father always says he came to this country because you could shoot for the moon. Anything is possible."

"Anything, Tadpole?"

"Almost anything, but … come to think of it, you'd better forget about Kiyoka. She's mine!" He tapped me across the side of my head, bounded up from where he sat and sprinted down the path, laughing.

Up in Rupert there were plenty of natives as well as whites and Japanese. I always thought people got along okay, although mostly they stayed with their kind. The Japanese pretty much kept to themselves in the fishing villages. Other than me, there weren't usually many whites or natives in Sikima unless they were there on business.

The place where everybody did come together was school. The Japanese and the Indians came flowing in from the forest and the little fishing villages, and the whites came in from the town. Everybody got along and there really wasn't much difference. Except for maybe in marks. The Japanese took their schooling very seriously. They worked harder, studied more, never missed days, even when they were sick, and they usually got the highest marks. Maybe this got a few people a little annoyed, but I figured it was only fair. Those who worked the hardest deserved to do best. Who could argue with that?

The Japanese always worked hard. When the salmon were running, they'd go out on their boats before the sun rose and stay out there until after the sun set. When they weren't fishing, they'd fix their nets, or till their little plots of garden between the rocks, or dig out those rocks to make their gardens bigger, or paint their houses. That was one of the biggest differences between my village and Sikima. Those Japanese didn't believe in letting any wood go free without a regular coat of paint.

My mother's people are more relaxed about life. I couldn't even picture any of them digging out a rock. They've learned to live around and with the rocks. It's not that they're lazy. They just don't spend time doing things like that. It's funny, my father seems stuck in the middle. He thinks the Japanese work too hard and the Tsimshian don't work hard enough.

What sticks in my head though aren't the differences, but the sameness. I've never met any group of people who aren't stubbornly proud of the way they do things, who don't think they are right and the others wrong.

.6.

"Can you go on a little trip?" my mother asked.

I eyed her without answering. A "little trip" could mean just about anything.

"Down to Rupert. Smitty is going down to pick up supplies. He asked if you could go and give him a hand. Are you interested?"

"Are you kidding? Sure!"

"He's leaving in ten minutes."

"Fantastic! I heard Rupert gets pretty exciting on a Saturday night."

"If you call a bunch of half-drunk men staggering around the streets exciting," she replied. "Grown-up men, if that isn't a contradiction in terms itself, acting like stupid little boys. You think they'd act so stupid if their wives or girlfriends or mothers were around?"

"You think Dad's acting up where he is?"

"Not your Dad. It's not in his nature to act like that. Besides, he's an old married man with a grown son. Most of these soldiers here are hardly old enough to shave."

"I'm old enough to shave," I noted, stroking my hand over the few straggly hairs on my chin.

"Almost. But for tonight, anyway, you aren't going to Third Avenue. The truck will meet the supply ship down off the main military pier. Before you go, make sure that eagle is okay. You feed it today?"

"Twice. Changed the water too."

"Is it doing okay?" she asked.

"All right I think. It's still pretty nervous when people get too close, but then again nobody is getting too close," I answered.

"Can't say I blame them. That bird could rip a man open pretty good. I hope you're being careful."

"I am."

"Good. Now you better get going. I don't want you to keep Smitty waiting."

I took off my apron, balled it up, tossed it on the counter and raced for the door.

"No kiss for your mother?"

"No time for kisses," I yelled back over my shoulder.

I could feel a wave of excitement across the base. People were talking loud, laughing, hustling around. Soldiers, hair slicked down, big smiles on their faces, spilled out of the barracks and anxiously waited for their buddies to assemble. There was a lot of good-natured kidding, shoving and playful conversation.

For the first time, I wasn't just watching, but felt part of it all. Maybe I wasn't going to be doing the same things, but at least I was going to the same place.

When I got to the motor pool, Smitty was already in the cab of the truck, the engine going. I pulled myself up on the step, opened the door and swung into the passenger seat. We were taking one of the big double axle trucks called a butter box.

"Good to see you, Jed," Smitty greeted me. "I appreciate your help," he said, taking a big bite from a candy bar.

Smitty put the truck into gear and it ground and jerked into motion. We bounced out of the big barn housing the vehicles and he cranked the wheel sharply to the right to turn us towards town. Coming up to the front gate, he braked the vehicle and I braced myself against the dashboard as he brought it to a complete stop. Two soldiers blocked our path.

"Hi, Smitty. Can you give us a lift?" one of them asked.

"Sure, climb on board."

They both circled around the front of the vehicle. The hood of the truck was so massive they both disappeared from sight as they rounded the front. They climbed in.

"Hi, Jed," one offered. His name was Rylance. I'd said a few words to him when we met around the camp. He was always friendly and Smitty said he was okay.

"Are you going into town to do a little hunting too?" the other one chuckled. His name was Murdock. He was a nasty piece of work, always talking too loud and bullying people. I always made a point of avoiding him, although he was always asking me to bring him something or other when he was in the mess hall.

"Hunting? In town?" I asked puzzled.

"Well, that's what we call it," Murdock replied.

Both soldiers were in their dress uniforms. They had "MP" patches on their helmets and carried nightsticks. The "MP" stood for Military Police and their job was to assist the local police with problems that developed with any of the soldiers.

"Maybe instead of helping Smitty tonight, we could convince you to bring along your gun and help us," suggested Murdock.

He made me nervous. I'd heard he had a bad temper and enjoyed busting a few heads, just for fun. That attitude, combined with his size, made him scary.

"If you think grizzlies and cougars are dangerous and unpredictable, you haven't seen anything until you see the drunks in town battling with each other," continued Rylance.

"Sorry, guys, he's with me tonight," Smitty said. "Besides, we can't have anything happen to Jed here. Between his hunting and his mother's cooking, he's the most valuable person in the camp."

Soon we turned off the unpaved, uneven road leading to the camp and onto the county road leading into town. Smitty geared up higher and the engine roared, this time much deeper, as we picked up speed. Looking to the side I saw we took up almost all the room and I was grateful there wasn't any other traffic on the narrow road.

"Where do you want to be let off?" Smitty asked the two MPs.

"Downtown, Third Avenue, right in front of the Royal Hotel," Rylance answered. "If that isn't too far out of your way."

"No problem. I figured that's where you'd want to be left off. It gets to be like the wild west there."

"Naw," muttered Murdock, "worse than that. I just hope everybody can hang on to their body parts tonight."

"Body parts?" I asked.

"Yeah. Last Saturday night one guy got his nose half cut off in a knife fight."

"Not to mention that other guy who had his ear bitten off," Rylance added. "Blood everywhere."

"Come on," I said, "quit kidding."

"He's not kidding, Jed," Smitty said. "I was on leave last Saturday night. There was one big brawl. Couple of those American sailors got fighting with a couple of natives. Fight ended when one of the Tsimshians ended up with a mouthful of American ear."

"That's disgusting."

"Sure was, kid. Blood everywhere. I think that injun would've scalped him next if we hadn't jumped in," Murdock chuckled.

"Indians don't scalp people," I said.

"No? Don't you ever go to the movies, kid?" Murdock continued. "Don't you know nothing about injuns?"

"Just what I'm told," I replied through clenched teeth.

"Then you're real lucky to have me set you right," Murdock thundered. "After breaking up fights every Saturday night, I'm an expert on injuns. An expert. Anyway, it serves that guy right. Any fool who would turn his back on a liquored injun deserves to lose his ear."

Smitty and Rylance were staring straight ahead, out the window. Murdock wasn't stupid. He knew my mother was native. He was trying to be an ignorant goof. Actually I didn't think he had to try very hard to be a big goof. It was probably a natural talent.

Turning on to Third Avenue, I could sense things would be getting busy before the night was out. Although it was only seven-thirty, there were already lots of soldiers, sailors, merchant marine and a smattering of locals, wandering the streets. Judging from the conversations floating in through the window of the truck, a few had already been drinking.

Smitty eased the big truck over to the side of the street, right in front of the hotel. The brakes squealed as it slowed down. Even before we'd come to a complete stop, Murdock flung open the door, climbed out onto the step and leapt to the ground.

"Have no fear, I am here!" he bellowed to a group of other MPs and a couple of RCMP officers who were standing there. I guess he wanted to make a big entrance.

Rylance turned to me and shrugged. "Don't waste any time on anything he says, Jed. He's just that way."

I nodded.

"Thanks for the ride, guys," he said and climbed down from the truck.

Smitty put the truck back into motion and we continued down the main street.

"He's right, Jed. Most people are pretty good about things. Others are just jerks. It wouldn't matter if it was

Indians or Germans or women or Martians. People like Murdock got to have somebody to hate. It makes it easier to bust their heads if he don't like them, and that's probably what he really likes, busting heads."

"How come jerks like him can always get away with it?"

"Not always, it just seems like always," Smitty answered. "Matter of fact I was thinking about beating the crap out of him myself.

I looked at Smitty in amazement.

"Course then I remembered he's big enough and mean enough to break me into little bite-sized pieces," he chuckled. "You got to remember there are other ways of getting back at people like him."

"What do you mean?"

"Well, let's say the next time he orders you around or demands something different from the kitchen, you know, like a hotter cup of coffee. You just take that cup, and when there ain't anybody looking, you just spit in it."

"Smitty!"

"Or put some dirt in it, or maybe a little pinch of pepper, or some soap," he continued.

"I can't do that! It wouldn't be right!"

"Sure it would be. Nothing wrong about giving a jerk like Murdock exactly what he deserves. Next time he bellows, 'Hey, boy, get me another coffee!' you just say, 'Yes, sir, right away, sir,' and then you take it into the kitchen and throw in a little of that stuff we put in the latrines. It would feel right. He's just like them toilets ... full of crap."

We both broke into laughter.

"But what if I get caught?"

"Don't get caught," he answered. The famous words of my Naani. "You know what the worst thing about Murdock is? He says he's mad about all them 'drunken injuns' but he's at least partly responsible for them being that way. Murdock is one of the biggest bootleggers around. He smuggles in booze and then he gets someone to sell it to the natives. He makes sure that nobody, none of the other MPs or police, bothers his guy while he's making all that cash selling the booze."

"How can he get away with it?"

"Easy," he shrugged. "Most people don't know, most of those who know, don't care, and those who know and care are too scared to do anything."

"Does Major Brown know?"

"No way. If the major knew, then old Murdock would be spending his time digging new latrines."

"Ever thought of telling?" I asked.

"Nope. Nothing worse than a snitch. Murdock will get what's coming to him, sooner or later, with or without me."

Coming up to the gatehouse of the dry dock, Smitty slowed down and again we came to a halt. A guard carrying a rifle on his shoulder came walking smartly out to meet the truck.

"Orders," the guard said curtly.

Smitty reached into his shirt pocket, pulled out some papers and handed them to the guard. He examined them and handed them back.

"Go straight down, turn right onto pier three. Your ship is docked at the end."

"Thanks," Smitty replied. He put the truck in gear one more time.

We rolled up to the ship, a supply vessel called the *Gypsy Rose*. It was a private boat under contract to the Canadian Navy to do non-military work. Almost all the ships that belonged to the Navy had been sent to guard convoys traveling to England. The few that remained were far too valuable to be used to deliver groceries.

"This is where you're going to earn your pay," Smitty announced. "Follow me."

We walked up the steep gangplank from the pier onto the ship. I looked up and down the length of the ship. There were no signs of life. It was completely deserted.

"The hard part is always finding somebody still aboard who can tell me what to pick up. As soon as one of these scows get into port, it's like rats deserting a sinking ship. The crew scurries off as quick as can be, anxious to see how fast they can spend their money."

"Somebody must be left."

"Maybe, maybe not. Sometimes I've had to just sit tight and wait."

We walked along the length of the vessel, moving towards the bridge.

"Heeelllooo!" Smitty yelled. "Heeelllooo!"

Up ahead a hatch popped open and a little man, old and hunched over, came out.

"Hi ya, fellas. What can I do fer ya?" he asked.

Smitty pulled the orders back out of his shirt pocket and handed them to the man. He unfolded them and stared for a long time like he was trying to memorize what was written there.

"So, you two fellas want supplies, is that right? Is that what you want?"

"Well, I want to meet a good woman and the kid here would probably settle for a new baseball mitt, but I think we better take the supplies," Smitty responded.

"What?" the old man asked in confusion.

"Just joking. We want our supplies. It's all written down on the requisitions."

"Requisitions?" the old man asked.

"Yes, you know, the papers," Smitty replied. "Those things you're holding in your hand." Smitty pointed to the orders the old man clutched.

He looked down and the expression on his face indicated he was surprised to see them there, and was unsure where they came from.

"Is there anybody else on board to help load the truck?" Smitty asked.

"Just me. I'm the captain, cook, crew and cabin boy when we hit port."

"That's what I figured." Smitty turned to me. "Well, Jed, according to our orders we don't have to unload the supplies. The ship's crew has to bring everything dock side. We have a choice. We can wait for somebody else to get back, we can load it ourselves, or we can make old gramps here move as much as he can before he keels over with a heart attack."

I looked at the old guy. I didn't think he could lift his own feet high enough to climb up a set of stairs. "Let's get lifting."

"Okay, gramps, can you show me and the kid where the supplies are?"

"Sure, sure, just follow me." He turned and went back through the hatch where he had originally emerged. "Try and keep up with me, okay," he chuckled.

I'd never been below deck on a ship as large as this. It was dim and I almost bumped my head as we passed through the first doorway. I figured the old fella had a real advantage being hunched up the way he was if all the doorways were as low as that one. We trailed after him as he went down a set of narrow metal stairs, and then along a thin walkway between wooden lockers. He stopped when he came to locker number seven.

"This is it," he said, opening the door.

I peered inside, and even in the dim light, was amazed. Boxes were piled right up to the ceiling. A quiet swear word escaped my lips.

"Let's have none of that, Jed. I'm in charge of both the driving and the swearing. You'll have to get a few years older before you can do any of either," Smitty scolded.

•••

Over the next three hours we moved supplies. The old guy had offered to help. He stayed in the back of the truck, and as we heaved up the boxes he arranged them. I was surprised to see how easily he muscled them into position. It was obvious he'd been doing this for years. Smitty and I exchanged glances.

"He's doing a good job."

"Yeah," Smitty said quietly, "probably working on instincts alone. It's like the way a chicken will run around for half a minute after you cut its head off. This guy has probably been doing this so long he'll be able to run the ship for two months after he croaks."

"Even longer than that," the old man said. He turned to face us. "Lots of things don't work as well as they used to, but the ears are still fine."

Smitty looked embarrassed. "I'm sorry," he stammered. "I didn't mean anything bad."

"That's okay, young fella. You's right anyway. After doing this for fifty-five years, they're going have to nail the coffin lid shut to keep me from doing my job."

Smitty hauled himself up into the back of the truck. "Either way, I was wrong." Smitty reached out his hand. "I'm John Smith — Smitty — and this young fella is Jed Blackburn."

I reached up and shook his hand.

"Pleased to meet you fellas. I'm Frank Bartlett. Folks just call me Bart."

"Well, Bart, we appreciate your help, and thank you for being willing to tolerate a fool and his young assistant."

"No problem. Tell me, kid, what kind of Indian are you? What's your tribe?"

My eyes opened wide with shock. "I'm Tsimshian. Part of me … I'm half Tsimshian."

"How'd you know that, Bart?" Smitty asked. "He looks

kind of Italiano to me."

"I wasn't going on looks. Going on the way he acts. Kid acts like he's native."

"Just how does a native act?" Smitty asked.

I was even more curious than him to hear the answer.

"Well, for one thing, he doesn't give an old man a hard time," Bart chuckled and Smitty looked embarrassed all over again. "Natives treat their old people good. But more than that, it was the way he looks at things, watches, listens. He stays still. Just look at him."

I had this strange desire to look at myself.

"Most whites I ever met think that silent is stupid and words, any words, is smart. Indians know better. Most of 'em only talk when they have something to say."

Smitty nodded in silent agreement.

"I always remember something my old man told me. He's been dead for forty years now, but I can remember his words. He said, 'Frankie,' he always called me Frankie, so he says 'Frankie, sometimes people think you may be dumb when you don't answer 'em, but it's when you open your mouth that they can know for sure if you really is or not.'" Bart started chuckling. "I figured it was always better to keep 'em guessing."

"Well, Bart, or should I say, Frankie, only a fool would think you were dumb," Smitty said. He smiled and put a hand on Bart's back. "But we better stop gabbing and get on lifting."

•••

It was almost 11:30 when the last box found its way into the truck. It was later than I'd thought it was going to be. I knew my mom would be worried. We shook hands with Bart and climbed aboard the truck. Smitty jockeyed it back and forth to turn it around on the narrow pier.

"I wonder how fast a truck like this would sink?"

Smitty asked innocently as the very back overhang of the vehicle was above the water.

"Let's not find out."

"Sure thing." With one more twist of the giant steering wheel, he finally aimed the truck in the right direction.

As the truck pulled up to the guard house the guard stood directly in our path, signaling us to stop. He rounded over to the driver's side and climbed up on the step. "I was asked to give you an order. You have one more pick-up before you head back to the base."

"Pick-up? Where?"

"The courthouse."

"Courthouse?"

"Yep. They're using it for a temporary holding area. I heard it's been a busy night in Rupert. Big brawl smashed its way clear out the front window of the Royal Hotel."

"So, what do they want with us?" Smitty questioned.

"Nobody told me. Just told me to tell you where to report," the guard replied.

"Thanks," Smitty grunted.

Pulling out of the port, we moved along a side street parallel to the main drag. All the houses were quiet, the lights out, no sign that anyone was awake. Smitty turned and we crossed over Third Avenue. Glancing out the window and down the street, I could see it was in sharp contrast to the surrounding streets. There were cars on the move, lights in all the windows, men — and some women — strolling along the sidewalks and over-flowing onto the edges of the road. Honking horns, loud conversation and even louder laughter filtering through the window and over the noise of our engine. Smitty brought the truck to a halt in the driveway in front of the courthouse. I grabbed the door handle, preparing to get out.

"No way, Jed, you stay here."

"Why?"

"Somebody has to guard the supplies."

"Guard boxes of canned food? Nobody's going to steal this load of crap!"

"Hey! Watch your mouth. Now just do what you're told. I thought Tsimshian were supposed to listen to their elders," Smitty chided.

"You're hardly my elder."

"Regardless. Stay put." He slammed the door shut behind him, and went into the small side door at the base of the courthouse steps.

From where I sat high up in the cab, I had a good view of everything. There were a few other vehicles in the driveway, two RCMP patrol cars and four military jeeps, one of which belonged to the American army. There were three American soldiers sitting on the steps of the court. Off on the grass there was a cluster of men. They were sailors in the merchant marine. I wondered if a couple of them were from the ship we'd just unloaded.

Smitty re-emerged. He held the door open and Rylance appeared. He was missing his MP's helmet and even in the dim light I could tell one of his eyes was swollen shut. Following behind him were men from our camp. They walked with their eyes on the ground. A couple had ripped or muddied uniforms. One was limping badly and leaning on his buddy. At the end of the line were two RCMP officers holding their nightsticks in front of them. The line slowed down and one of the Mounties poked the last man in the back with his stick. He didn't even turn around to protest.

With the last person out, Smitty let go of the door and ran to the front of the line. "Jed, help me get the tail down."

I jumped down from the truck and joined him at the back. Together we untied the canopy and lowered the tailgate.

"All right, everybody get in," Rylance yelled. It

sounded much more like a pleading request than an order. Wordlessly they started to climb into the back, taking up positions against the boxes of canned goods. The air was thick with the smell of alcohol. Some of the men looked like they'd been dragged behind a horse. Blood stained some of their white dress shirts. The last man, of the fourteen I counted, climbed aboard.

"Seal 'em up," Rylance said.

We raised the heavy metal tailgate and it squealed in loud protest. The canopy was pulled into place and the ropes tied down to the back hooks.

"Okay, guys," Rylance said to the RCMPs. "I'll have the major call your commander and they can figure out together what to do with this lot."

One of the police officers turned to Smitty. "Make sure you hit every bump between here and the camp. Maybe you can knock a little sense into them."

Smitty nodded in agreement and we climbed into the cab of the truck. I sat in the middle and Rylance sat by the window.

"I'm going to drive like I was carrying newborn babies," Smitty responded.

"Why?" asked Rylance. "The way these guys acted tonight they deserve what they get."

"I'm not thinking about them, I'm thinking about me. As it is, the back of the truck will smell bad, but if I'm not careful the whole thing will be floating in vomit. Do you know how hard it is to get rid of that smell?"

"I can imagine," Rylance chuckled, "but I wouldn't worry about it. There's going to be lots of guys to scrub trucks. These men will be on punishment duty right through this war and into the next one."

"What happened?"

"It all started small. A couple of our guys and a couple of natives. It got out of hand quick. By the time it was over, there must have been over two hundred guys fighting. Locals, Indians, merchant marine, US sailors, some American soldiers, our guys. Everybody fighting everybody. The RCMP and us MPs were waist-deep in it, but we couldn't get it to stop."

"Wow," I gasped.

"Murdock must have been in his glory," Smitty noted.

"Actually, he spent most of the time face down in the gutter."

"Murdock! What happened?"

Rylance shook his head slowly. "I almost had it all sorted out and then Murdock comes busting in swearing and pushing and acting like a big shot. He pushed this guy, a little guy, an Indian, and the guy decides to push back. Before I knew it Murdock is toppling over like a redwood." A smile came to his face. "It was the only part of the evening I enjoyed."

"You didn't happen to take any pictures, did you?" Smitty chuckled.

Rylance burst into laughter and then grabbed his jaw. "Ooooww, that hurts … please, no more jokes."

"Or maybe you could re-stage it and we could sell tickets," Smitty continued.

Rylance started chuckling again, his hands still on his jaw.

"Anybody seriously hurt?"

"Nobody died. A minor stab wound. A couple of concussions. Of course, when these guys wake up to-morrow, between the hangovers and the major, they might wish they had died."

.7.

Reveille. I rolled off the couch, stood up and went to the window. It was still dark out, as usual, but somehow it seemed to be a deeper dark. The trumpet continued to blare away, louder and longer, and it almost sounded angry. After getting in so late with Smitty last night, I spent the night at the base. My mother came out of her room.

"Why doesn't somebody tell him to go back to bed?" she muttered. "Doesn't he know what time it is?"

"What time is it?" I asked.

"Four-thirty."

"Four-thirty! Why so early?"

"Beats me. I'd better get dressed and start breakfast, it looks like things are beginning earlier than usual today." She went to get changed.

I pulled on my shirt, buttoned it up and slipped into my moccasins. Outside I could hear people stirring and moving around. There were voices yelling out directions. I opened the door and moved out onto the walkway. The air was cool and goose bumps exploded on my arms. I leaned against the railing. It was sopping with dew. On the parade ground I saw outlines in the thin dim light spilling out of the windows of the barracks.

Within a few minutes there was complete silence. The men were assembled and stood at attention, waiting. Nobody dared move or speak. I sat, quietly, feeling like if I breathed too loudly everybody would turn in my direction. The silent vigil went on for about fifteen minutes before a lieutenant emerged from the major's office. He walked along the walkway, the sounds of his boots echoing off the surrounding buildings. He stopped on an elevated section directly overlooking the parade grounds where the men were assembled.

"At ease!" he ordered.

There was a shuffling of feet but no other noise.

"The following men are to report immediately to the mess hall."

He started to rattle off names. I went in to offer my mother some help in setting up for breakfast. I figured I could slip in quietly and hear everything that was going to be said during the meeting.

"I'm back. What can I do to help?"

"You mean, what can you do so you can hear what's going on, don't you?"

"Well … can't I do both?" I replied.

She smiled at me. "Take the trays and the plates out. Walk quietly. Don't look at them no matter what. Ignore them. Just pretend nobody's there. Okay? Do you think you can do that?"

"Sure, no problem. I know how to ignore people. I'm a teenager. I'll just pretend it's you telling me to do something."

"Smart-aleck kid."

I heard the front door open and the sound of boots scuffling along the wooden floor. I picked up an armful of trays and went into the dining area. Sitting at the far end, together at a single table, were the soldiers I'd briefly seen last night. I looked at them out of the corner of my eye. I put down the trays and turned back into the kitchen. Walking back with my second load of trays, I saw the whole group had their eyes trained down on the floor or table top. There was a barely audible murmur of conversation. I'd been pretending they weren't there, but now I realized they were praying they were some place else. I heard the door open.

"Attention!"

Their chairs scraped against the floor as they jumped up. I perked up my ears as I disappeared into the kitchen.

"At ease. Please be seated," Major Brown said. "I will not be mincing my words, gentlemen. You are all in significant trouble. I have arrived at an understanding with the local RCMP commander, in a late night meeting, to withdraw any pending criminal charges. I convinced him that any punishment I shall mete out to you will greatly exceed anything the courts would impose. And believe me, gentlemen, that was not simply a promise but a total guarantee. Does anybody have anything to say for themselves?"

There was no answer.

"I asked, does anybody have anything to say for themselves?" he said again, this time in a much louder, more stern voice.

"No, sir," came a soft response. "No excuses, sir," another offered.

"Good. Perhaps you couldn't act as soldiers last night, but you will take your punishment as soldiers. I have received the initial estimates for the damages done. This includes a new plate glass window for the Royal, a dozen broken chairs, and damages to an RCMP patrol car. The total cost will be equally divided amongst you fourteen gentlemen, starting with your next pay. But you won't be needing money because there is nowhere on base to spend money and none of you will be seeing anything except this base for the foreseeable future. I direct you now to the bulletin board where you will see your work assignments posted. Dismissed."

The men shuffled out of the mess hall. The door

closed and then, silence. The only sounds were the skillet sizzling in the kitchen and my moccasins softly meeting the floor. Major Brown looked up at me as I re-entered the dining area with another load.

"Jed, do you think you could get me a coffee?"

"Yes, sir."

My mother must have heard his request because as I entered the kitchen she was already holding a cup. "He takes it hot, black, no sugar," she said quietly.

I carried the mug back to the major's table and set it down carefully in front of him. He was staring down at the table. I turned and started to walk away.

"Jed."

I stopped. "Yes, sir?"

"What did you think of all that?"

"All what?" I asked, feigning ignorance.

"Come on, you're neither deaf nor dumb. What did you think of what went on in Rupert last night?"

"It's not my place to say anything."

"But it is your place to answer a question. I'm asking a question."

I swallowed hard and thought harder. He sat there, staring up at me, waiting.

"I don't understand all of it," I said. "I only know the bit I saw by accident last night, a little bit I was told, and what I overheard today. It wouldn't be right for me to give you an answer without knowing more."

He took a long sip from his coffee. He put the cup down very deliberately and looked directly at me. "That is probably the smartest thing ever said in this mess hall. Mid-day there will be a meeting here, between me, the RCMP commander and one of the Tsimshian elders, George Star. Do you know him?"

"I've met him a couple of times. He was a friend of my grandfather. Sometimes he'd come by the house."

"Do you think he can be helpful in sorting out some

of our problems?"

"Everyone says he's really smart. He's well respected. The Tsimshian listen to him."

"Good, then it was wise to have him be part of this meeting. I would like you to stick around and hear what is going to go on at the meeting. Maybe after that you can answer my question."

My mother came out of the kitchen and motioned for me to start working again.

"I'll try, sir. Is there anything else, sir, or can I get back to helping my mother get ready for breakfast?"

"Please, don't let me take you away from your work. You and your mother are the only two people in the whole camp, including myself, who I know for sure are actually doing their jobs well. That reminds me." The major turned to face my mother. "Mrs. Blackburn, do you think it's possible to get a few more people to hunt for us? I'll give them the same offer as your son's."

"Does that deal include jackets as well? Jed's cousins have been eyeing that jacket of his."

"That should be no problem. An army issue jacket for each of them."

"Then it might be possible. Probably not any of the men, though. Too busy working down in Rupert. Some of them have two or even three jobs. But, I'm sure one or two of Jed's cousins would be interested."

"Excellent, excellent!"

"While we're talking help, I could sure use an extra hand in the kitchen."

"That shouldn't be difficult. I know of fourteen candidates for the position," Major Brown said firmly.

"Nope. Rather have no help than that help. I want somebody who's there by choice."

"Somebody like Jed?"

"Yep. Another helper like Jed."

"Arrange it," Major Brown agreed. "Arrange it." He

rose and left the mess hall.

Mother answered with a smile and went back into the kitchen to continue getting breakfast ready. I followed in after her.

"Any ideas who can help?" I asked.

"Couple. Maybe Jonnie … maybe Peter."

"How about Tadashi?"

"Tadashi? I didn't know he could hunt."

"I'm sure he can," I replied, although I was pretty sure he couldn't. I knew he didn't even own a gun, but I could loan him my old rifle. "But I know he'd be good here in the kitchen. He's a hard worker, polite, and does what he's told and …"

"Sounds good. Maybe I should hire him and get rid of the guy I've got helping me now."

"Mother!"

She started laughing. She had the most wonderful laugh, and it wasn't just me who thought so. My father and mother met at a Legion dance. He'd told me how he heard her laugh float across the room. He couldn't see her, just hear the laugh. He trailed after the laughter until he saw her. She kidded him that it wasn't love at first sight but love at first sound.

"Talk to your cousins tomorrow. I guess you won't be seeing Tadashi until school on Monday."

"Couldn't I maybe go and talk to him later today? Maybe after supper?" I'd been spending so much time at the base that I really hadn't seen much of Tadi and I missed him. "It would be nice to have him hanging around here with me."

"Hanging around? Don't think I'm hiring anybody to hang around."

"You know what I mean," I protested.

"Go, right after you help with meal prep. I know you've been missing him."

"Thanks. It's going to be great to have him around."

"Don't count your chickens just yet. How do you know he'll even be interested?"

"He can use the money," I answered. I knew he was saving for university.

"We'd better finish getting things set. Have you taken care of your eagle this morning?"

"I'll do that right now," I said.

"Good. It's bad enough I've got all these men to feed without me having to go out there and take care of that bird when you're not here."

•••

It didn't take us long to clear up after the lunch crowd. It was a smaller than usual gathering since there were two squads of men who were either deep in the forest digging a new garbage pit, or working on the road leading out of camp. Rather than warm lunches, they'd be eating meals packed when they left after breakfast.

At a few minutes to two, Major Brown entered the mess hall. He walked around absentmindedly before coming back into the kitchen.

"Mrs. Blackburn, could you please put on a fresh pot of coffee?"

"Sure thing, Major. I just finished baking a berry pie. Still hot, sitting there on the window sill, cooling down. How about I bring out a piece to all three of you?"

"That won't be necessary," he answered. "These gentlemen are coming here for a serious discussion, not a social tea."

"A little food never hurt anything. Good food can get rid of a lot of bad tastes."

"Tsimshian logic?" he asked.

"It works."

"I'm sure it does. Do we have any ice cream, maybe vanilla, to go along with it?"

"I'll see what we can do."

At precisely two o'clock the door to the mess hall opened again and in strode the commander of the local detachment of the RCMP. His polished boots made a staccato sound as he moved across the hall to shake hands with the major.

"Good day, Major," he said formally. "I trust you had an opportunity to get a few hours sleep after our meeting."

"A few, just a few."

The commander looked at his watch. "I don't suppose our friend has arrived yet. I've yet to meet an Indian who's ever been on time."

From the way he said "friend," I could tell the commander considered George Star to be something else. I did know what he meant, though, about him not being on time. It drove my father crazy when one of my mom's relatives would show up hours, or days late, or simply not come at all after saying they'd be there. The Tsimshian aren't really too interested in clocks and being on time.

I stayed out of sight in the kitchen. I could hear the two of them talking quietly but couldn't make out any of the words. I sat down in front of a mountain of potatoes needing to be peeled before supper. About fifteen minutes passed before I heard the front door open once again. I was glad George had finally arrived and sneaked over to peek out through the kitchen doorway. To my surprise I couldn't see George. Or the commander. Major Brown sat by himself at the table, his back to me.

He turned and saw me. "You might as well come out, Jed, there's nobody else here."

I walked out and he turned around. "Well, Jed, that certainly wasn't very helpful."

"No sir," I answered, looking away.

"Could you bring me two pieces of that pie, Jed?"

"Two?" I questioned.

"You do want the second piece, don't you?"

"Yeah, definitely," I said enthusiastically.

"Good. See if your mother also wishes to join us."

Major Brown was like two different guys. When the men were around he never smiled, or joked or acted friendly. All of the men respected him. Some even feared him. When there was nobody around, though, he was completely different. His face softened, his walk and talk slowed and he smiled. I bet there were people, lots of people, in this camp who figured he didn't even know how to smile. My mother said this was the "real" man and not to take the other side of him too seriously, he was just doing his job.

I returned to the kitchen. My mother plunged a knife into the pastry and a puff of steam escaped into the air. I told her what the major had asked and she cut two pieces, putting them on plates and then onto a tray. She next took a big spoon and scooped out some vanilla ice cream and placed it on the top of the two pieces of pie. She handed me the tray and walked ahead.

"That smells wonderful, Mrs. Blackburn, just wonderful."

"Thanks. You'll find that it tastes even better than it smells," she responded, taking a seat across from him.

"Coffee, sir?" I asked.

"Please, Jed," he said motioning to me to sit. "I think I can help myself." He got up from his seat and walked to the kitchen where my Mom kept the big coffee urn.

He had no sooner left when the door to the mess hall opened. George Star peeked his head in the door. It had been a couple of years since I'd seen him and he was a lot older than I remembered.

"Naomi! Jed! What a surprise to see you two here," he said as he came into the room. He moved slowly with a limp.

"Good to see you, George. Major Brown told us you were coming," my mother said. "I'm the cook around here and Jed helps out and does a little hunting."

"The major … that's the fella I'm looking for."

"He's in the kitchen, getting himself a coffee. Want one?"

"Sure, that would be nice."

"What you want in it?" she asked.

"Black, lots of sugar."

"Hey, Major!" my mother yelled. "Can you bring another coffee … black … plenty of sugar!" She turned to George. "How's the family?"

"Can't complain. Oldest grandson hurt his leg some working over in the cannery, but most are doing good. And how's your family?"

"We're all well. Mom is doing well, busy like always."

"You make sure you say hello to her for me. Wise woman. I hope you listen to her stories, Jed. You'll learn a lot about our people, a lot about yourself," he said.

I liked listening to my Naani's stories, but I didn't understand how he figured I could learn anything about myself from them.

"There's some chill in the air this morning. When November starts this way it's going to be a cold winter ahead," George said.

"That's just what Naani was saying," I added.

Major Brown came back into the room carrying two coffees. I caught the look of surprise and then saw his face transform. His smile vanished and he put on his "Major" face. His steps became shorter and sharper and he straightened his back.

"Thanks, Major Brown," my mother said. "That second coffee's for George here. You two haven't met, have you?"

"No, we haven't," Major Brown replied, extending his hand to shake.

George rose slightly from his chair and shook hands. "Good to meet you, Major. I'm George Star. Thanks for the coffee," he said as he raised the mug to his mouth.

"Do you think there might be some space alongside that coffee for a slice of pie?" my mother asked.

"I think there might."

My mother rose from her seat. I got up as well. I went to the corner to start getting things ready for the supper rush.

"The commander left. You are almost an hour late," Major Brown stated formally.

George shrugged his shoulders.

Mom returned with two pieces of pie. She put a generous slice in front of George and a smaller, second one by the major. Both thanked her and she disappeared back into the kitchen.

"Bad scene in Rupert last night," George commented.

"Definitely. A number of my men, as well as a number of others, including some Tsimshian, were hurt. I think we have to do something before somebody gets more seriously hurt or even killed," Major Brown said.

"Makes sense. Do you have any ideas?"

"I would like you to talk to the Indians about not drinking. It is against the law."

"If you don't want 'em to drink any, you shouldn't sell 'em any."

"I cannot control all of the bars and hotels and moonshiners in Prince Rupert, Mr. Star," the major answered curtly.

George took another long sip from his coffee. "I was just hoping you could control your men. The biggest bootleggers in town all seem to be wearing Canadian army uniforms."

"My men! That is absurd! Do you have any proof to back up these serious accusations?"

"Just a bunch of drunken Indians, and who believes a bunch of Indians? Nobody talks to 'em, just takes their money, busts 'em on the head and throws 'em in jail."

There was silence as they drained their coffee cups.

The two men sat, staring at each other. I cleared out of the dining room and through the door to the kitchen.

"Here," my mother said, pushing a tray into my hands. "Bring them more coffee."

"I can't go back in there."

"Do what you're told," she said, quietly, but with a cold look of authority in her eyes.

I walked into the room, carrying the cups of steaming coffee, careful not to stumble. I was afraid to breathe. Both men looked in my direction as I stopped beside them.

"Coffee?" I asked as I stood before them.

"Thank you, Jed," Major Brown answered.

"Thanks, Jed," George said.

I put the coffee down on the table and each man took one.

"Good coffee," George noted. "Your mother's put a little bit of seasoning in here, hasn't she?"

"I think so. Something Naani picks from the forest."

"So you've been doing some hunting."

I nodded my head.

"We're very grateful to have both Jed and his mother here at the camp."

I smiled and felt my face get a little flushed. My mother entered the mess hall and started setting out the trays and plates for dinner. I went over to help.

"Mr. Star, I give you my word, my personal word, I will look into this accusation. If liquor is being spread through my camp, it will be dealt with. I am going to talk to my men. You have my word."

"That would be good," George replied.

"I will also talk to the men in general, and my MPs specifically, to discuss the way they handle the Indians. I'm going to make sure they realize they are here to protect the people, all the people, and that includes the Indians."

"Ahh … protect us from what?"

"From invasion, of course."

"A little late to help us there."

"What do you mean?"

There was silence. I knew George was taking his time before answering. This might have been because he was thinking, or more likely, to show respect for the question and the seriousness of the answer. My grandfather had explained to me once that natives think a quick answer to a question shows disrespect for the person who asked the question.

"You got to understand, Major, for us the invasion happened a hundred years ago. We were our own nations for thousands of years before any whites came to this continent. So Japanese or Canadian army doesn't make much difference."

"Surely you cannot compare the two. Have you not read or heard of the things the Japanese are doing as they've swept across Asia?"

"I've read some. It may be different, kinder here, but the same in the end," George answered. He got up from his seat and slowly walked over to the window facing the parade grounds. He pulled back the curtain and stared out.

"Don't think I've ever seen an eagle like that, all tied up," George said. "Where'd it come from?"

"It was wounded by gunfire," Major Brown explained. "It was found on the outskirts of camp two weeks ago, hungry and dying. The men brought it in. We feed it. It's become the unofficial mascot of the camp." The major got up from the table and moved over to the window.

"And I bet you people treat it pretty good. Feed it, protect it, things like that," George continued.

"Yes, it is treated well. Jed here, along with his mother, is mainly in charge of it."

"I'm sure Jed's doing a fine job. Still, I bet it snaps at

people, doesn't want them too close."

"Well, yes, it is a wild creature," Major Brown conceded.

"That's right, a wild creature. Meant to be flying around these mountains, not tied down to any pole. Treat it good or bad, it don't matter none, it still wants to be free. I got to go now," George said.

"But we're not through talking," the major objected.

"I am. Talked more today than I like. Thanks for the coffee and pie. Jed, Naomi, take care of yourselves and say hi to your family."

"Mr. Star, we have things that need to be discussed, decisions to be made."

"Tell ya what. Tomorrow or the next day, you come and see me and we'll talk." He turned and left. Major Brown remained at the window. My mother and I looked at each other. She walked over and stood beside him.

"I just don't understand these people," he said.

"Do you want to understand?" she asked.

"Of course, I do!"

"Major, you've always treated Jed and me good. With respect. It's important to show people respect."

Major Brown smiled at her. "So you're saying I didn't give George any respect. Is that right?"

"Of course," my mother explained. "You hardly gave him any respect. Since he's an elder of our tribe, he should be shown complete respect. Like you'd show to a general."

"Can you tell me what I did that was so disrespectful?"

"Well, you wanted to meet with George and then you ordered him up here."

"I didn't order him to come!" Major Brown objected.

"Of course, you did. You sent some soldiers in their jeep to tell him to come here. Even if they did say please, and they probably didn't, it was still an order. Then when he does come here, the first words out of your mouth are to scold him for being late, and then you call him a liar when he tells you that your men are selling booze to the locals."

Major Brown nodded. "That all wasn't too bright, I agree, but that wasn't all of it, was it?"

"No. I knew there'd be trouble when he saw that eagle."

"What about the eagle? We're just trying to nurse it back to health. We couldn't just leave it or it would have died."

"You're probably right. But, sometimes it's better to die free than live all chained up like that. Isn't that what this whole war over in Europe is all about?"

"Why … why … yes it is," Major Brown frowned.

"Eagles are important to our people and especially to our clan. Jed and me and all our family are part of the eagle clan. Our ancestors can take on the form of eagles when they pass over. You may not believe it, but we do. We see an eagle up there and we think good things. Not just that it's powerful or free or beautiful, but maybe that it's watching over us. We honor them, we don't go shooting them down out of the sky."

Major Brown looked away.

"You got to remember my people feel like that eagle chained out to your flagpole. We've had so much taken away; so much that belonged to us is gone, forever." There was a pause, a long pause. "Now, all that seems left to some of them is to snap and claw and fight. Like the eagle."

He shook his head slowly. "I wish we'd had this conversation before I had the meeting. Things might have had a better chance to come out all right."

"It's not too late. He likes you," she replied.

"He likes me! You must be joking."

"Nope. He didn't end the meeting forever, just for today. He gave you an invite to come and see him. That's important."

The major smiled, just a little, but he smiled.

"And Major, you'll do better."

"Do you really think so?"

"For sure," she answered. I could see a smile flowing from her eyes. "It has to be better than this meeting."

.8.

"The carrots are all cut up. What should I do next, ma'am?" Tadashi asked my mother.

She eyed his finished pile and then looked at the one I was working on, still only half done.

"Hmmmm … it looks like I didn't need a second helper … just the right first helper."

Tadi broke into a big grin and I shot them both a dirty look.

"Start taking the piles of plates off the counter and set them out in the mess hall."

"Yes, Ma'am," Tadashi answered. He grabbed a stack and pushed through the door to exit the kitchen.

"You could learn from him, Jedidiah."

"How to cut up carrots?"

"No, manners. Tadashi is polite."

"He's not polite, he's Japanese. It just comes natural to them," I countered.

"Don't know about that, but I do know it comes more natural than cutting carrots does to you. Here, give me the knife and I'll finish up while you help Tadashi get things set up in the mess. Okay?"

"Sounds good to me."

I dropped the knife into the bowl of carrots and handed it to her. I grabbed another stack of plates and headed out of the kitchen. Tadi was almost finished putting out the plates he'd brought in.

"Come and give me a hand with these, will ya," I called out.

Tadashi put down the last of his plates and joined me.

"I'll hold the stack and you put the plates on the table."

"Okay."

"And one more thing. Could you stop being so polite?" I asked.

"What do you mean?"

"Polite, polite. Quit being so polite ... it's making me look bad. Okay?"

"Yes ... sir," he chuckled.

I smiled. "That's more like it."

"I just want to make a good impression. Don't want to get fired my first day on the job."

"What do you think about working here?"

"I like it. Money's good and the company is, you know, okay."

"Okay! Just okay? If I wanted to be given a hard time, I would have asked Toshio to work with me!"

"Hah! I can't picture Toshio wearing a Canadian army jacket."

"What's wrong with the jacket?"

"Nothing. I just think the only uniform he'd wear would be from the Japanese Imperial Army."

"He wants to be in the Japanese army?"

"Well, probably not. It's just he's always talking about how the Japanese army is doing in China. He practically memorizes the stories in the Japanese newspapers."

"You mean newspapers come all the way from Japan to your village?" I asked in amazement.

"Some of the old people still do get newspapers shipped from Japan. It takes months for those to arrive. But I mean the Japanese newspaper published in Vancouver. It comes out once a week and takes another week or so to come this far north."

"I don't understand why people would come all this way, thousands of miles from Japan, to still be so interested in what's going on back there."

"People have relatives in Japan. Besides, like my father says, 'Just because someone moves their body doesn't mean they move their heart.'"

"Are there many people like that ... you know ... whose hearts are still in Japan?"

"Mostly the people born in Japan."

"Your father was born in Japan. How does he feel?"

"He says he didn't travel halfway around the world to stay in the same place. That's why he became a Canadian citizen."

"Just like my father. He moved here from England to become a citizen."

We set down the last of the plates. "Now we have to fix up the big urns to make coffee. Come on and I'll show you how." He watched as I took off the tops, filled them with water and measured out the coffee.

"Think you can do that?" I asked.

"Not too tricky. You know it's not the same."

"What's not the same?"

"Your father and my father becoming Canadian."

"What do you mean?"

"For one thing your father enlisted and is fighting in the war."

"Yeah?" I questioned.

"My father couldn't do that if he wanted. They don't let people of Japanese descent enlist in the army."

"You're kidding, aren't you?"

"Nope. If you're Japanese you can't join the army. I may be the only Japanese in all of Canada who is wearing one of these jackets."

"But that doesn't make any sense," I argued.

"Of course, it doesn't. It's just that ..."

Tadashi stopped talking as we heard the outside door

to the mess open. We both turned around. Major Brown came into the room followed by a group of his officers. Included in the group was Captain Stevenson, the second-in-command on the base. I eyed Stevenson nervously. I didn't like him. As an officer he was supposed to order people around. But he was always making sarcastic little comments. He didn't treat the men very well and it wasn't just me who didn't like him. He figured because he outranked people he was better than them. Smitty told me the army was full of people like that.

Major Brown looked over at us and gave a quick nod of his head. The group sat down at a table in the corner.

"You see what my mother wants you to do now, and I'll go and see what I can get the officers," I whispered to Tadashi. He nodded and walked to the kitchen. I walked over and stopped at the end of the table. The major was seated with his back to me. Captain Stevenson was facing me. He looked up.

"Coffee, black and hot and plenty of it," he barked.

"Yes, sir," I answered and spun around on my heels.

"Jed!"

I stopped and turned back. The major had swiveled around in his seat.

"Yes, sir?"

"We have some special guests tonight. I was wondering if there's any chance of some rabbit pie?"

"Not from me. I'm here all afternoon, but my two cousins went out hunting first thing this morning. They should have no trouble bringing back enough game."

"Excellent! I'm not surprised to see your mother arrange things so quickly." He turned and cast a disapproving gaze at Captain Stevenson. "If only the rest of my orders were followed so promptly."

Captain Stevenson looked down at the table.

"I'll get the coffee now, sir."

I turned away before the smile came to my face. I

liked to see Stevenson get into trouble, but didn't want anybody to see I liked it. I hurried into the kitchen.

"Tadi, can you help me bring out some coffee?" I asked.

"Sure."

I handed him a tray and piled on cups. I grabbed the coffee pot and we headed through the door. The men were engaged in a spirited dialogue as we approached. I set down the coffee pot and then took the cups off the tray, putting them in front of each officer.

"This is the perfect time to introduce our newest mess assistant," Major Brown said. "This is Tadashi Fukushima. He is a close friend of Jed's."

"But he's Japanese!" Captain Stevenson exclaimed.

"I think we're all aware of that," Major Brown calmly replied.

"Although more correctly he's Japanese-Canadian. How long has your family been in Canada now, Tadashi?"

"About thirty years, sir."

"And as I recall you mentioning, your father's a naturalized Canadian."

"Yes, sir."

"Interesting. I've only emigrated to Canada twenty years ago myself, so I believe that would make him more Canadian than …"

The door burst open. "Major Brown, sir!" called a soldier. "The call you were waiting for is on the line, sir."

"I'll be right there!" he answered. "Gentlemen, please have your coffee and I'll be back promptly." He got up and hurried out the door.

I started to pour the coffee.

"I would hope you have your registration card with you," Captain Stevenson said to Tadashi.

"No, sir … I don't have a card."

"You don't have a card! The law is quite clear that all Japanese need to be registered and carry their card with them at all times!"

"I'm only fourteen. I don't have to be registered."

"Oh … oh … I thought you were sixteen years old … I have trouble telling the age of you people," Captain Stevenson sputtered. "You two can leave. If we need anything more, we'll call."

I put down the coffee pot on the corner of the table and we hurried away.

"Nice guy, hey?" I said as we entered the kitchen.

"Captain Stevenson being difficult?" my mother questioned.

"About the same as usual. What was he talking about? What's all this business about registration cards?"

"All Japanese over sixteen years old, even people born in this country, had to register with the RCMP," said my mother. They were all given little registration cards they carry with them at all times."

"You know about this?" I questioned.

"I'm surprised you didn't know, Jed," she replied. "It's pretty common knowledge."

"But why would they register the Japanese?"

"In case there's a war with Japan," Tadashi answered.

"Enough of this. Upsets me just to hear about it. You two better stop wasting time talking if you expect to get to Tadi's for supper tonight. Is it some sort of special meal or something?"

"Yes, ma'am. It's my grandmother's birthday celebration."

"Well hurry up and finish setting up for supper and then you can be on your way."

"No problem, we'll be finished in plenty of time," I answered.

"And don't forget about the eagle. You have to feed him and change its water."

"Already done," I replied smugly. "First thing when I got here."

"I should've known. I wish you'd take school as serious as you take caring for that eagle."

"I take school seriously enough. Besides, Eddy needs me."

"Eddy? What kind of fool name is that for an eagle?" my mother asked.

"Seems all right to me. The men gave it a name, that's all."

"Bad enough keeping it all tied up like that. Least they could do was give it a proper name," she insisted.

"What did you have in mind?"

"I don't know. A Tsimshian name. Something the eagle would like."

Tadashi shot me a questioning look. My mother caught his expression and he looked away in embarrassment.

"The Tsimshian think that our people can become eagles after they die," I explained to Tadashi.

"And don't you go making any fun of things you don't understand, Jedidiah Blackburn."

I knew better than to argue with her, or even be a wise guy when she addressed me by my full name.

"You just better make sure that if I ever get hurt you treat me as well as you treat that eagle. Understand?"

"Yes, ma'am."

"Good! Now get back to work ... the both of you!"

●●●

Tadashi had been quieter than usual the whole rest of the afternoon and all along the walk to his village.

"Hard day's work, eh?" I questioned.

"Not too hard."

"I thought you were all worn out."

"What makes you think that?" he asked.

"You seem too tired to talk."

"Not tired. Just bothered."

"Bothered about what?"

"What do you think?" Tadashi asked. There was just a hint of anger in his voice. He stared straight ahead up the trail and seemed to pick up the pace a bit.

I had to think for a few seconds before it came back to me. "Don't let Stevenson get to you. He's a jerk with everybody."

"Maybe, but it's not just him."

"Then what?"

"The registration. It isn't right we have those little cards to carry around."

"I don't know. From what you've told me it isn't a bad idea to have somebody like Toshio registered. He'd give the Japanese the maps to Prince Rupert if he had them," I chuckled.

"I don't care about Toshio. Maybe he should be watched, but not all of us!" Tadashi's voice was still calm but now he was setting a faster pace.

"But you don't even have a card, right?"

"Yeah, but only because I'm not sixteen." He was still staring straight ahead, not looking at me. I had to speed up to try and stay even with him.

"So you have to carry around a card, so what? I don't know, but it doesn't seem like that big a deal."

"You're right … you don't know," he said angrily. "It *is* a big deal."

"The government is just taking precautions because of the war. Don't take it so personal."

Suddenly he stopped walking and turned to face me. "How else could I take it? It is personal. Everybody who's Japanese, or whose parents or even their grandparents were Japanese, has to register! It's like we're not humans and we need a piece of paper to go out.

"Come on, Tadi, you're making too much of this."

"No, I'm not! Think about it. How would you like it if you and your family had to register?"

"Me and my family?"

"Yeah! What if your mother and grandmother and you had to carry around those little cards with you wherever you went? How would you like that?"

"I guess I wouldn't," I admitted. "But why would they register us? I was born here and my father's a Canadian citizen, and …"

"Just like I was born here and my father and mother are naturalized Canadians. My father's been in this country longer than your father! Why don't they make your father register? What's the difference?" he demanded. "What's the difference?"

I stood silently. "I don't know … there isn't a difference, I guess. I just wasn't thinking about it … I'm sorry … I just didn't understand."

The fire in his eyes faded away and his shoulders slumped down. "I'm sorry too. I didn't mean to yell at you. It's not like it's your fault. You're not the guy who made up all that stuff."

"That's okay," I replied. "I should have been smarter about it."

We started walking again.

"And anyway, you're right … they wouldn't make your father get registered no matter what. He's English and white. But, if things were different, I could see how they might make your mother and grandmother and you register."

"What are you talking about?" I questioned.

"They don't treat the Tsimshian much different than they treat the Japanese. I heard some of the bars and hotels in Rupert don't even let natives in, and they can't buy liquor and things like that."

"Yeah, but still, that's different than all that registration stuff. My mother's people have been here for thousands of years … thousands," I responded. Now I started moving slightly faster.

"Your mother's people? Why do you always call them

'your mother's people'? Aren't they your people too?"

"What are talking about?" I asked. Tadashi was lagging behind.

"The Tsimshian aren't just your mother's people. They're your people too. You're Tsimshian too."

"I'm Canadian is what I am. Canadian!"

"The way I figure it you're at least half native, so if they ever decided to register the Tsimshian, there'd be a fifty-fifty chance they'd make you register and ..."

"Shut up!" I yelled, turning to face him. "Shut right up!"

"Come on, Jed, I was just trying to ..."

I turned away and started back up the path. I could hear Tadashi's steps trailing behind me. Now I wasn't in any mood to talk.

●●●

"Was it difficult today working?" Mrs. Fukushima asked, as we took off our coats in her warm kitchen.

"Not too bad," Tadashi replied. He picked up a couple of plates and took them to the table in the other room. Yuri smiled shyly at me, but said nothing as she moved from the counter to the table with food.

Mrs. Fukushima nodded her head slowly. "You both seem ... tired."

"We're more worn out from the walk home," I said, without telling her the reason why the walk was so tiring. We'd walked in silence for quite a while before we started talking about other things and pretended we hadn't had words.

I went to grab a steaming bowl from the counter.

"No, no, Jed. You are our guest," Mrs. Fukushima said.

"Here, let me take it!" I turned around and Midori was standing in the doorway, a big smile on her face. She walked over and gently took the bowl from my hands.

"Please, Jed, will you join my father and mother at the table."

"Yes, ma'am."

"Come on," Midori said, holding the door to the dining area open. "You can sit beside me."

Tadashi came through the open door back into the kitchen, as Midori went the other way into the dining area. I wondered if he'd heard her comment. He came up beside me. "Oh, no, Jed," he murmured in a girlish voice, "I would just die if you didn't sit beside me." He started to laugh. I looked at Yuri and could see that she was having a hard time holding back as well. As I turned and left the kitchen, I heard her start to giggle.

Mr. Fukushima was seated on the floor at the head of the table. Etushi's grandmother was sitting to his side. They were speaking in Japanese but stopped when I entered. Mr. Fukushima motioned for me to take a seat on the opposite side from where Midori and Yuri would sit. I squatted down and sat on the right hand side of the table, two spots down from him. The place between us was reserved for Tadashi. Mrs. Fukushima would be at the end of the table, although she would never actually sit down during a meal.

I reached out a hand and stroked the wood of the table. Their table always intrigued me; smooth, shiny wood, polished to a gleam; black with an intricate pattern of painted flowers. There was something beautiful about the table. Tadi always said he'd take a real table with long legs and chairs any day of the week.

The table was fully set. A series of small plates; square, rectangular, oval and round sat on the table in front of us, looking so small and delicate that it made me think of a dinner party for dolls. Each plate was for a different type of food. Beside the plates was a tea bowl. Sweet green tea would be served throughout the meal.

Midori and Yuri came in carrying two more platters of food which they placed in the center of the table along with the two large covered bowls. They sat down at the

· 105 ·

table, followed by Tadashi. Mrs. Fukushima entered last and immediately began serving the steaming rice.

"We are honored you could join us on this special celebration," Mr. Fukushima said quietly.

"Thank you for having me."

"Special food for a special occasion," Midori added.

I could see some of my favorites already adorned the table. Aside from the rice, there was sushi and wakame. Thank goodness I'd eaten wakame before I knew what it was — a type of seaweed tied into a bow — or I might never have found out how good it tasted. There was also a platter holding food I didn't recognize.

"What's that?" I asked, pointing to the unknown dish. It looked almost like a jelly roll except it was steamy white, veined with lines of red.

"Kamaboko," Mrs. Fukushima answered.

"Steamed fish," Tadashi translated. "The red lines are made of soy beans. One of my favorites. We only get it on special occasions."

"Like birthdays," Tadashi's grandmother smiled.

"And engagements of marriage, and weddings and wedding anniversaries," Midori added.

"I see," I answered. She was really starting to make me nervous.

A long time ago Tadashi had explained to me that, to the Japanese, eating is as much about ceremony as it is about putting food in your mouth. There's a tradition to the way things are cooked, presented on the platters, put on separate plates and eaten. Appearance, the way the food looks, mattered as much as taste. And, no matter how wonderful something tasted, you were never to take very much. Small pieces of many, many courses made up all the meals.

•••

During the course of the meal Mrs. Fukushima only

joined us at the table for a few minutes. Most of the time she worked in the kitchen, brought in the dishes, or served at the table. Midori and Yuri had now joined in and were clearing the table. Even Tadashi's grand-mother was helping clear things away.

"Saki," Mr. Fukushima requested. His wife nodded in acknowledgment.

"For three?" Tadashi asked, giving me a sideways glance.

"One," he replied. "Only one here to have saki. Next you will be asking for shouchu."

"What's that?" I asked.

"It's like saki except instead of being made from rice it comes from fermented potatoes," Tadashi explained.

"A little stronger," his father added.

"A little stronger!" Tadashi said with a grin. "A lot stronger, and it doesn't taste nearly as good as saki."

His father gave him a puzzled frown. "How would you know about the taste?"

Tadashi looked as if he would have crawled under the low table if there were room. "I … I … just …"

Mr. Fukushima started laughing and the tension and nervousness dissolved. "I tasted both before my time, without my father knowing, too," Mr. Fukushima said. "Midori!"

She popped her head out of the kitchen. "Yes, Father?"

"Bring three cups for saki."

"Three?" she questioned without thinking and then thought better of it. "Yes, Father." She disappeared into the kitchen.

"Perhaps the time is now for the two of you. Both are working hard … earning money for your families."

Mrs. Fukushima entered carrying a ceramic decanter. Inside was the heated saki. Yuri followed and placed a small cup in front of each of the three of us. Mrs.

Fukushima poured the saki, first for her husband, then me and finally she filled Tadi's cup. She left the room.

"We are most grateful for your assistance in arranging our son's position ... and for your friendship. I wish a toast."

I lifted my cup. The smell from the saki floated up to my nostrils. It was sweet and fragrant. It smelled like plums.

"To the gold that is family and the silver that is friendship."

I brought the cup to my mouth and took a sip. It was warm and strong tasting and burned as it blazed a path down my throat. I coughed and gagged a little. I could feel Tadashi smiling beside me. I tipped back the cup and took a bigger sip, suppressing the urge to cough again.

"And to boys who are becoming men," Mr. Fukushima said, raising his cup again.

I drained my cup. I wondered what my Naani would think about me drinking rice wine. She had no use for alcohol. I guess she didn't have to find out everything. I glanced at my watch. It was almost eight o'clock, well after the time I'd told her I'd be home.

"I have to go. Thank you for the meal," I said, as I rose to my feet. My legs felt a little rubbery.

Tadashi and his father got up as well.

"I will come part way with you to your village," Mr. Fukushima said.

"That's okay, I can go on my own."

"No. A walk after dinner is good."

"Yeah, a walk would be nice," Tadashi agreed.

"You have school work to complete," his father stated firmly.

"I've finished all my homework."

"Have you finished learning all you can learn?"

"Well ..."

"Then stay. Work, study, practice. I will walk with Jed."

Mr. Fukushima got ready while we all said our good-byes. Tadi walked me to the door.

"Why is your father coming with me?" I asked quietly. "He's never come along with me before."

"I think he wants to talk to you."

"About what?"

"Beats me," Tadashi shrugged.

I was never completely comfortable walking through the forest alone after dark, so I should have been grateful for the company. Instead, I found myself less nervous about the things that could be lurking in the darkness than I was about why he was here with me. We covered a good part of the distance between Sikma and my village in silence.

Finally he spoke. "You and Tadashi are good friends."

"The best."

"And you will always be friends ... never less ... but never more."

I didn't understand what he was getting at so I walked along in quiet confusion.

"Friends. You will always be a friend to my family. To my wife and to me ... to my son and to my daughters. To Midori. A friend. Nothing less, and nothing more."

We walked along in silence for a while.

"I should turn back for my home," Mr. Fukushima said quietly. "Remember you are always welcome in my house and at my table."

"Thank you."

"But also remember we can share a meal and a pathway, but in the end you will go home to your village and I must go home to mine. Good night, Jed."

"Good night."

I watched him walk away into the darkness. He was invisible within a few dozen steps, but the sound of his footfalls echoed for a few seconds.

His words echoed on in my head much longer.

.9.

"Okay, spit it out," Naani ordered.

"Spit out what?"

"Not your food. The only thing you done with your fork is push it around the plate. None of the food has found its way into your mouth."

I glanced down at my meal, still all there but piled up high at one side of the plate.

"Something's eating you so hard you can't be eating anything else," she continued.

"Can't a guy just not be hungry?"

"Maybe, a guy, but not this guy. Besides it's more than eating. Your spirit's been all wrong since you came back from Tadashi's house last night."

"My spirit?"

"Yep, your spirit. You got something hurting inside, I can see it right through your hide."

I held up my arm and turned it around. "You must be seeing things, all I see is skin."

"You're looking in the wrong place. I wasn't thinking it was your arm that got hurt but your heart. What happened? Did you and your friend get in a fight?"

"Well, yeah, a disagreement, but that all got settled … more or less."

"Then what?" she persisted.

"Nothing."

"Nothin, or nothin you want to talk about?"

"Nothing … it's nothing important … it's stupid."

"If it was stupid, you could eat, your spirit wouldn't be wrong," she reasoned. "Must be important."

"Well it's just … I can't understand … It just doesn't make sense. I don't know where to begin or how to do this."

"Start at the beginning. You talk. I listen." She smiled and placed an old wrinkled hand on top of mine. "I'm here to listen. Remember, whatever it is, I probably been down the same path some time in my life." I looked into her soft, warm, brown eyes and knew that what she was saying was true.

"It has to do with something Mr. Fukushima said to me."

"He's a good man … can't see him say nothin hurtful," she responded. "Least ways, not on purpose."

I nodded my head slowly in agreement.

"But he said something that upset you. What?"

"Well, you know how the Japanese are, they don't talk directly at something, they kind of talk around it."

"Like the Tsimshian."

"Yeah, like the Tsimshian," I agreed. "At the end of the meal he told everybody he wanted to go for a walk, so he came part way home with me. He talked about family, and the future and things like that."

"Important things."

"It's just I think what he was saying was I could always be a friend of the family, but I could never be family, that my future and his children's future are going to be different."

"He's a wise man. Probably right. Your future will be different than Tadashi."

"And Midori."

"And all of his children. Why Midori 'specially?"

"He doesn't want me to marry Midori," I said looking away.

"He said that?"

"Well, not really, he just talked around it."

"I didn't even know you wanted to marry her."

"I don't!" I answered forcefully.

"Then you and Mr. Fukushima agree."

"No, we don't. I don't want to marry her, but he doesn't want me to marry her."

"Sounds the same to me."

"No, you don't understand. He doesn't think we can get married because she's Japanese and I'm not."

"She is Japanese and you're not."

"But that shouldn't be a reason we can't get married. If we like each other and we want to get married, then we should be able to."

"Should be able to," she agreed.

"Why doesn't he think I'm good enough for his daughter?"

"I didn't hear you saying that he said that. I think he said the two of you are different, and you are."

"Well, I know, but that doesn't mean we can't get married."

"Of course, it don't, Jed. Maybe what he was saying was that it wouldn't be wrong, but it would be harder."

"Harder?"

"Yeah, harder. Not as easy. People on both sides, people from either side, give you trouble. They don't understand and think you're wrong. Kids from the marriage come out somewhere in the middle, sometimes feel like they don't belong anywhere."

I felt my face flush and my tongue suddenly felt thick.

"You know about that, Jed. You know about being in the middle. Does it bother you?"

"No!" I barked, and pushed myself away from the table. The chair legs squealed against the floor and the dishes rattled. I was tired of people always bringing this sort of stuff up. I didn't feel in the middle of anything.

I looked at my Naani and she appeared surprised by my response. The anger of my answer had shocked me as well. I sat down again and took a deep breath.

"I'm sorry," I apologized.

"Nothin to be sorry about. Just remember I'm your Naani, Jed. I was there when you were born, when you were in diapers, when you first went to school. I know you're almost all grown up, fourteen, a man to the Tsimshian, but I still remember that little boy coming home from school crying because them boys called you an injun. I still remember."

I hadn't thought about that for such a long time.

"I told you not to worry, cause them boys was right. You were half injun. Nothing wrong with that, is there?"

"I guess not, I mean no ... it was just the way they said it was all ... just the way they said it."

"They said it like it was something wrong."

"Yeah."

"And that's how you felt today when Tadashi's daddy was talkin to ya."

I nodded my head.

"He don't mean nothin by it, Jed. He just wants what's best for his kids. Wants to save them from havin to do things the hard way. Don't mean nothin bad about you. Nothin at all."

She rose from the table and started to clear away the plates. I followed her example, piling dishes on top of each other. I'd gotten pretty good at carrying plates over the past weeks. My plate, still covered with food, rested on the top of the pile. She disappeared into the kitchen carrying her load.

"Stop!" Naani ordered me. "Stand right there."

I stopped, my hands full of dishes, in the doorway between the kitchen and the living room.

"Jed, can you see the kitchen?"

"That's a pretty stupid qu ..." I started to answer

before she cut me off.

"Don't smart mouth an old woman. Can you see the kitchen? Yes or no?"

"Yes," I replied.

"Can you see the living room?"

I turned my head to look over my shoulder to where I'd just come. "Yeah."

"Are you in the kitchen or the living room?"

I looked down at my feet. One foot rested on the wooden floor of the living room while the second was on the linoleum of the kitchen. "Both. I'm in both."

"That's a good answer. You're in both. You coulda said neither but you said both. People born between two cultures are like you standing between two rooms. You belong to both, you see into both and you can understand both."

I lifted up the foot that rested on the wood and placed in on the linoleum. My Naani watched.

"Simple as that you can walk into one room or the other. You can be part of both."

"Or," I said hesitantly, "part of neither."

"You's a smart boy. Take after your Naani. Or part of neither. Some people in the kitchen think you belong in the living room, and some people in the living room think you belong in the kitchen. They're wrong. You belong anywhere you want. Anywhere!" Her high-pitched voice echoed off the kitchen cupboards. She never yelled and I was startled.

I put the dishes down on the counter.

"When Mom brought home Dad, did you think they should get married?" I asked.

"I wasn't too sure at first. Your Grandfather knew. No way he thought they should marry."

"Because my Dad was white?"

"Nah. Your Grandfather was a typical father. He didn't think anybody, white or native, would be good enough for his daughter. I was a typical mother. Just knew it would be harder, and I didn't want my baby to go through anything hard. You got to remember, Jed, and you probably won't know this 'til you're a father with grown children, that your children are always just your babies. Even when they're all grown up, kids of their own, living alone, big important jobs. You still remember them being in diapers, falling down, having to make the tears go away. Your mother is still just my baby."

"So you didn't think they should get married, either?"

"I didn't say that. I worried, but I knew they loved each other. They fit together good. Real good. Their spirits were right for each other. I knew it should be. It'll be that way with you too, someday. I'll be able to tell. Just make sure to bring all your girlfriends here to meet me, and I'll let you know the right one."

I felt myself turning red. Somehow I just knew she was right.

"'Sides, we're Tsimshian and Tsimshian always marry out of their clan. Eagles marry Ravens and Ravens marry Eagles. As soon as the marriage takes place the husband becomes part of the wife's clan. Just the way your grandfather left the Raven clan of the Haida to marry a Tsimshian Eagle. And with your father being a pilot and named Blackburn, I figured for sure he was a Raven. So an English Raven married your mother who's a Tsimshian Eagle. Now your father is Tsimshian."

"I don't think my father would see it that way."

"Don't matter how he sees it. Facts is facts."

"Did Grandfather see it the same way? Did he accept my father as being part of the family? I know they were always arguing about things."

"Your Grandfather would argue with a tree if it would answer him back. That was just the way he was. It didn't mean nothing. He came to respect and even love your father. He watched the way your father always treated your mother and you. Your father may think that he's English, but I know he's Tsimshian. He just has to lose that funny accent." She turned away from the dishes in the sink with a smile on her face. "Now, go out, call on Tadashi and leave me to do the dishes in peace."

I hesitated.

"Well, what is it?" she asked.

"I'm feeling hungry all of a sudden. Do you think I could get something to eat?"

She took her hands out of the sink and flicked a fine spray of water and soap in my direction. "Get out of here," she playfully yelled, chasing me out of the kitchen. "But don't go too far. I'll call you back for a snack after I'm finished washing up."

.10.

"Mom, I'll be back in a while," I said, slipping on my jacket. "I have to feed Eddy."

She turned away from the stove and looked at me. "Feed him what? You didn't take any food."

"I've got a rabbit."

"Where did you get a rabbit?"

"Shot it on the way over here. I left it outside."

"Why did you do a fool thing like that? Bring it in and I'll make the major his favorite stew."

"Can't do that. Rabbit is Eddy's favorite too."

"Yeah, but last I checked, that eagle wasn't paying you to hunt. Bring it in here and I'll be able to pay you for it. Give him some meat scraps instead," she suggested.

"Meat scraps aren't as good as a rabbit."

"Why not? What difference does it make to the bird?"

"A lot. It's important to give him fresh kills … things he'd usually eat. If I feed him table scraps, he'll turn into a house pet and he'll never be able to fend for himself," I explained.

"Silliest idea I ever heard in my life. Who told you such a thing?"

I smiled knowingly.

"Naani. It was Naani who told you, wasn't it?"

I nodded.

"I don't know anybody who knows more about eagles than your Naani," my mother admitted. "Quit standing around jawing and go and give your eagle its rabbit, and do it quick before the major finds out about it."

I went out through the back door. My game bag, its flap closed, was just off to the side where I'd placed it. I picked it up and slung it on my shoulder. I looked all around. There were a few men milling around, but Major Brown was nowhere to be seen. I made a beeline straight for Eddy.

I was about halfway across the parade ground when I skidded to a stop. Up ahead, sitting on Eddy's perch was Naani. Eddy was sitting only a few feet away on the top of his little house. I rushed over.

"Naani, what are you doing here?"

"Sssshhhhh!" she hissed loudly at me. "Don't you got no manners? Don't go rushin in and interrupting us like that."

"What do you mean, interrupting us? You shouldn't be sitting that close …"

"Ssshhh!" she hissed again, turning around to glare at me. "Either sit down and be quiet or go away, ya hear?"

"But …"

The glare in her eyes sharpened and I closed my mouth. I sat down on a stump just beyond reach of Eddy's tether.

"Now where was I?" she said. "Oh, yeah. So Stoneribs he so happy to be given a killer whale skin that he puts it on and swims out into the ocean. He swims far, very far. He's enjoyin being out there swimming around … enjoyin his new clothes … enjoyin being a blackfish. He's jumping and bobbing and diving and having hisself a great time. And the morning turns to day and the day turns to night and he keeps on swimming and splashing. But Stoneribs isn't noticing nothin but the water and the fish and the seals. He don't notice it's now dark and fog has rolled in. He stands right up on his tail and pushes his head out of the water as high as he can, but

· 118 ·

he can't see nothin. He can't see the shore. Stoneribs feels all tired. Don't feel like he can swim anymore. Don't know if he can even hold hisself up." She stopped and turned to face me. "And don't you go and tell me that a whale can't get tired."

"I didn't say anything," I said in my defense, holding up my arms.

"But you was thinkin' it."

She was right … again.

"Stoneribs wasn't a real killer whale. He just a boy wearing a killer whale skin and boys get tired, right?" she argued.

"Of course."

"Good! Now back to the story." She turned around to face Eddy. Eddy tilted his head to one side and stared at her like he was waiting for her to continue. "So Stoneribs is getting more and more tired. He don't know which way to swim. No matter how hard he looks, he can't see the shore. He can't see and he's gettin more tired and more tired, and he thinks he'll never get a chance to see his home again … that he'll just sink under the waves. And then he hears it. Real faint at first, but then it comes again. The cry of the eagle.

"Stoneribs feels a little stronger and looks all around. He can't see nothin but he hears the cry again so he swims in that direction. The eagle keeps crying and Stoneribs keeps swimming 'til finally he sees the shore, and he climbs out of the water and takes off his killer whale skin. He looks up and sees the eagle sitting on the branch of a tree. Stoneribs tells the eagle he will not forget what he did. And he never did." She stopped talking and there was silence.

"Is that the end?"

"'Course not. Stories don't end. Ever. Just where I'm stopping for today."

"Could you do me a favor, and move a little farther

away from Eddy?" I said anxiously.

"Why?"

"I don't think you should be that close. Nobody sits that close."

"Why?"

"Because he can hurt you."

"Him?" she asked incredulously. "He never hurt me before!"

"Before? When were you up at the camp before?"

"Here? Never. First time today."

"But you said he's never hurt you before so that means …"

"Married to him for nearly fifty years. Knew him for fifteen years before that."

"Naani, come on …"

"Don't you be going on. I'm not gonna waste my breath convincing you. Hard enough time convincing him," she said, motioning to Eddy. "Old fool can't remember nothin. Must'a had all the sense knocked out of him during the *chaanug*."

"The *chaanug*?"

"The fall, the fall. When he fell from the sky, he hit his head, lost his memory," she paused. "And speaking of forgetting, why don't you remember any Tsimshian anymore? You used to speak some Tsimshian when you was little. Now you don't speak none."

"I remember a few words."

"Then why don't you speak none of it? Just a word every so often. Why don't you do that?"

"Could we talk about this someplace else? Maybe we can go and see Mom."

"Sure thing."

I felt a wave of relief as she ambled out of Eddy's range.

"Come on, Mom's right over here," I said. I took a few steps and then stopped. "Wait! Hold on a second, I have to feed Eddy." I lifted up the flap and pulled out

· 120 ·

the rabbit by its long back legs. I dropped the bag to the ground.

"Here, Eddy," I called and tossed it to him.

Naani nodded her head enthusiastically. "Good to see ya listenin to your Naani and feeding him good things."

Eddy jumped down on the carcass. He tore a large strip off and tossed it down his gullet.

"Hah! Look at him go! Told you it's your grandfather ... you know how he always love rabbit."

"All eagles like rabbit. That doesn't mean this eagle is grandfather."

"How come you think he's not your grandfather? Just look at him! Sittin up there with that look in his eyes, not talkin but ready for a good old fight. Besides, why you think he's here?"

"Because he was shot down and they found him in the forest and brought him here."

"Wrong! He's here to look after you and your mother. Sitting up there on his perch he can see everything that goes on. Just here to take care of you!" She said the last few words so loud a couple of the men working close by turned to stare at us.

"Okay, okay! Fine, he's here to take care of us," I said quietly, placing my hands on her shoulders. "Can we go and see mom now? Please."

"'Course." She turned to the eagle. "Be good, you stubborn old man. I'll come back another day and tell you the story about the boy who fed the eagle."

We started towards the mess again.

"Did you have any trouble getting on the base?" I asked. The major had been tightening up the security.

"Nope. No problem."

"Did you explain to the guards you were my grandmother?"

"Didn't say nothin to guards."

"But they had to ask you why you wanted to come into camp. They don't just let people wander in."

"Didn't talk to nobody. Saw some soldiers stomping around in their big boots making more noise than a moose in rutting season, puffing on their stinkin' cigarettes, and talkin away to each other. I didn't want to talk to none of them so I made myself invisible."

"You made yourself invisible? Like see-through, like a ghost or something?"

"Come on, Jed. Nobody but spirits make themselves invisible. I mean I just stayed in the shadows and moved slow and easy. Don't be goin silly on me, Jed … invisible," she said, shaking her head in disbelief. "Now where's that mother of yours?"

We walked across the parade ground and came up to the side door. I held it open for Naani. I reached down to my side and realized I'd forgotten my game bag.

"Mom's right through there," I said. "I've got to go back, I left my game bag by Eddy."

"Get it later."

"No, I have to get it now. What if somebody takes it or something?" I questioned.

"That old thing? It's so old and worn I can't see nobody makin off with it unless they think it's a rag for the garbage!"

"No. I have to go and get it."

"How about you just throw it away and I'll make you a nice new fancy one?"

"No, I want that one."

"What's so special about that old bag?" she asked.

"Nothing … it's just that it … it belonged to grandfather."

"Come to think of it, it did look familiar," she said, nodding. "I was always on him to let me make him a new one."

"I'll just be a second."

Naani went in through the kitchen door and I ran back across the parade ground. Of course the bag was still lying there on the ground. It wasn't like I'd left a pile of gold sitting there. I bent down and picked it up.

I looked at it. Naani was right. It was beaten up and worn. I wondered how many rabbits or ground hogs or whatever had found their way into this bag. I slung it on my shoulder and thought about it hanging on my grandfather's shoulder as he walked off into the forest.

I looked up to see Eddy glaring at me.

And for just a second, I thought I saw my grandfather's eyes staring back.

"Not enough to put on a sweater."

.11.

The knock on the door signaled it was time for me to
get going. I let the spoon clank down in the soggy remains of the cereal and got up to answer it. My Naani
moved away from the sink where she'd started cleaning
the breakfast dishes, and went to the ice box to get my
lunch. I opened the door.

"Good morning," Tadashi said. "It's a bit cool out
there today."

"You better put on something else if it's cold," my
Naani stated.

"He said cool, not cold. Besides, this is pretty warm,"
I replied, looking down at my army jacket.

"Your friend there has on the same jacket and he
says it's cool. At least put on something underneath. A
sweater or something. I feel cold."

"So let me see if I get this straight, old woman. You
feel cold, so I should put on a sweater? It's a good thing
you're not tired or I'd have to take a nap."

She burst out in a loud and raspy laugh.

"Now wait while I get it." She disappeared into my
bedroom and returned quickly with an ugly sweater. I
couldn't conceive of ever being cold enough to wear
that particular piece of clothing. I took it from her and
stuffed it in my knapsack. She gave me a nasty look.

"Don't worry, I've got it if I need it."

Her look got nastier. I went over, bent down and

gave her a kiss goodbye. Her face transformed into a smile.

"You're not very good at being mad," I chided her.

"Not enough practice, I guess."

Tadashi made a motion for me to hurry.

"We better get going, you wouldn't want to make us late for school," I said.

"Late, early, I don't understand what the difference a few minutes make. You not catching a boat. School will still be there a few minutes after nine o'clock."

"Well, until they make you the vice-principal, I think we better get going. I'll be home right after school. I'm not going to the base tonight."

"Good! You been spending more 'an enough time there. And you, there, Tadashi, when are you coming over for a meal? You haven't been here for three weeks or more."

"I've been busy with Jed at the base, but I'd like to come soon."

"Good. Soon. Now both of ya better get moving."

We both gave her a hug and left.

"Come on, we better hurry," Tadashi said and we broke into a trot.

The others kids from both villages were well ahead of us. They were already around the bend in the path and out of sight. Neither of us necessarily cared about walking with the group, but we knew they were on pace to get there on time. Unlike my Naani, the school did think being late mattered. One late was all you were allowed each term. Second late meant staying after school. Third late meant the strap, and I'd already been late twice this term.

Rounding a couple of curves, we soon found ourselves out of breath but within ear and eyeshot of the last few kids strolling along at the end. One of these was my "dear friend" Toshio. He turned around in time to see us sprinting up. He said something in Japanese, and then the other two kids walking with him turned towards us. All three burst into laughter.

"What did he say?"

"I don't know," Tadashi replied.

"Don't give me that," I snapped, "your Japanese is great."

"Yeah, my Japanese is fine but I couldn't hear him. He's too far away."

The three of them stood on the path, waiting and laughing. Two of them moved slightly off to the side to allow us to pass while Toshio remained rock still, forcing both of us to turn ever so slightly sideways to get by him. Almost immediately after we got in front of them, they started to follow, dogging our heels, still chuckling. I heard Toshio say something else that was greeted with another hail of laughter. I spun around to face him and looked at him, eyeball to eyeball.

"Jed, don't," Tadashi said, pulling at my arm. "He's too stupid to bother with."

"Hey, Toshio," I challenged, "it must be nice to have somebody laughing at something you said rather than at something you did. So what's so funny?"

I knew he understood a lot more English than he spoke, so I figured he'd get the insult. He mumbled some more Japanese and then all three chuckled.

"What did you say?" I asked again.

Toshio gave a broad smile. "I tell my friends that when you two run toward Japanese in your Canadian uniforms, that was last time any see Canadian soldier not running away from Japanese."

"Nobody's running from any Japanese."

I felt my cheeks flush and my hands curled into fists. I didn't care if he was older and maybe knew some of that judo; I was bigger and stronger.

"All Pacific Ocean, everybody running from Japanese," he taunted. "Canadians just scared children, like you. Soon they'll be running too."

I took a step toward him and Tadashi locked me in a bear hug. "Don't do it, Jed, he's not worth it."

"I'll show him who's running from who," I snapped at Tadashi as I forced my way out of his grip. "Let me alone!"

He suddenly released his grip and, caught by surprise, I stumbled forward. Toshio shifted quickly to the side and stuck out his foot. He hooked me behind the leg and I smashed down on the ground, landing hard.

There was a chorus of noise; laughter mixed with yells and gasps. I rubbed my hand against my face and was shocked to find it covered with blood, my blood. I wiped my hand on my pants and then bounced back to my feet and charged him again. He ducked down and I tumbled right over top of him, landing on my back behind him. The air rushed out of my lungs, and I felt a searing pain shoot down my back and into my legs. I tried to get back to my feet, but my legs gave way. Tadashi was at my side and helped me stand up.

"Come on, Jed, that's enough, just stop."

I could hear Toshio hurling insults at me. The kids who had been far ahead of us had all come back to watch. My cousin Jonnie came over and stood beside me.

"If you want, Jed, either me or Peter will finish this," he said. "He's a lot older than you." He was just trying to give me an excuse to allow him to fight for me without me losing face. I could picture Jonnie getting into it — he always liked a good fight — but Peter, who was as strong as an ox, and not much more talkative, never fought anybody.

"No, it's my fight."

"Listen, Jed," Tadashi said very quietly, "if you think you have to fight him, at least fight him smart. He's using judo. He needs you to charge at him. Don't. Get him mad. Make him come to you. Then you can pop him good. Understand?"

I nodded in agreement.

"Good, 'cause if you can't out-think Toshio, then you deserve to get the stuffing kicked out of you."

Jonnie and Tadashi let go of my arms and I walked toward Toshio. He was smiling, jabbering away at me in Japanese. I wanted to wipe that smile off his face and my urge was to rush him again. Instead I stopped just out of arm's reach and stood, my fists up. His smile faded when he realized I wasn't going to make it any easier for him. That made me more confident.

"Come on, Toshio, you stupid goof, I'm right here. Ya scared? That's it, isn't it, you stupid goof, you're scared!"

Now he looked confused.

"Toshio, nothing but a chicken boy." I tucked my arms under and started flapping them like they were wings. I strutted my legs, up and down, and made sounds like a chicken. "Toshio is chicken boy, come and get me chicken boy."

He looked angry and I could see he was fighting against himself to come and get me.

"You got him going, Jed," Tadi said quietly from behind me. "Make him squirm, really insult him."

I thought about what I could possibly say to get him going, to make him lose his cool.

Then I remembered the things that soldier had said to Tadashi to get him so mad.

"Toshio is fish-head … little yellow devil … slanty eyes … come on, you stupid little Jap … what a Nip … chicken nip!"

I could see it was working. His eyes became darker and angrier.

"Come on, you chicken … come on slanty eyes …"

Toshio roared with anger and then rushed toward

me. Suddenly, he yelped in pain. He turned part way around. Midori had hit him, across the back of the legs, with a branch. I bet that would put a serious crimp in the marriage plans. I leaped forward while his attention was directed to her and connected with a solid right to his face. He stumbled back and, before he could regain his balance, I hit him with another right. He went down. I started to move in again. Now that he was down, I wanted to really clean his clock.

"Enough!" my cousin Peter shouted, and all the other yelling stopped. Peter stepped in between us. He was so big he blocked Toshio from my view. He reached over, and with one hand, pulled Toshio to his feet.

"Go," he quietly instructed and Toshio staggered off, held up on both sides by his friends. He had blood flowing from his nose and mouth. Good! They moved off toward school, followed by a host of others.

I was surrounded by a group of kids, offering me congratulations. I still felt a little woozy. I looked around for Tadashi.

"Where's Tadashi?"

"He went with the others," Jonnie answered.

Typical Tadashi, I thought, shaking my head. He didn't want to be late for school, so couldn't wait around to help pick up his best friend. Peter made me sit down for a minute to clear my head before he'd let me go. By the time we left, the others were out of sight.

We got to school just at the bell and hurried in to take our seats. I didn't have a chance to talk to anybody. I took my seat and found I had even more trouble than usual paying attention.

At lunch time I wasn't particularly hungry and had a headache. I asked if I could go to the office and lie down on the couch in the nurse's room. I felt tired and closed my eyes.

"BBBRRRRRIIIINNNGGG!"

My eyes shot open and I caught sight of the clock on the opposite wall. It was 3:35, time to go home. I'd been asleep the entire afternoon!

I hurried down the hall, grabbed my things, and went out to meet Tadashi. He wasn't there. I guessed he thought I'd gone home already. Quickly I moved along the path, hoping to catch him. Within a few minutes I'd caught up to some of the kids from our two villages. I passed kids from Sikima; kids I knew, but nobody spoke to me. They barely said hello. I knew most of the Japanese kids thought Toshio was a jerk, but I seemed to be the one getting the cold shoulder.

Up ahead I saw Tadashi. I broke into a run and called to him. "Tadi!"

He turned around, but then turned back and kept walking. I sprinted up and stopped right beside him, panting.

"Sorry, I wasn't there to meet you," I apologized.

He walked on without responding. I figured he was mad at me because I'd fought Toshio.

""I guess I should have listened to you and just ignored the jerk," I offered.

"Did you say 'the jerk' or 'the jap?'"

"What?"

"You know, the jap ... the nip ... the fish-head ... yellow skinned slanty-eyed jap!" He spat out the words. He looked as angry now as Toshio had during the fight.

"But ..." I stammered, "I was just trying to get him mad at me."

"Well, you did that. You got a whole lot of us mad at you!"

"You told me to get him going ... I just didn't know what else to say."

"You could have insulted his mother, or said his father was a drunk or told him you were going to marry Midori! You didn't have to say all that other stuff."

"You know I didn't mean any of it," I pleaded. "I was just … I was just … I don't know …" my voice trailed off. "I'm sorry."

"Sorry isn't enough. Go away. I need to be by myself, to think."

"But, Tadi …"

"Go now, or you'll have to fight another fish-head."

I stopped dead in my tracks and Tadashi continued to walk. He moved farther and farther away, moving, not looking back. Stunned, I remained frozen in place while he disappeared around a curve in the path.

It didn't make any sense for him to be like that. It wasn't like I'd said any of those things to him. Why was he so mad …?

Injun … red-skin … savage … half-breed. The words came rushing back to me. I'd said the same things I'd had said to me. I felt sick to my stomach. My head spun.

I heard the sounds of kids coming up on the trail behind me. I hurried off. I was too ashamed to talk to anybody. I needed to be alone too.

.12.

"What's wrong?" Naani asked.

I hung my jacket on the hook without answering.

"No use ignoring it. I could feel your spirit's all wrong the instant you put your hand on the door. What's wrong?"

She was spooky sometimes. "I got into a fist fight on the way to school this morning."

"And?"

"And what?" I asked.

"And what else … more happened than a fight. Remember, telling only half the truth is the same as lying, only sneakier."

I nodded my head. "I said some things during the fight that got Tadashi mad."

"You were fighting with Tadashi?"

"No, of course not. I was fighting with Toshio."

"And what did you say?"

"I didn't mean any of it … it was just talk to get Toshio angry."

"What did you say?" she asked again.

"I insulted the Japanese … called them names."

She nodded sympathetically and placed her hands on my shoulders. "You made a mistake, Jed."

"I know … I just feel so … so …"

"Bad? Ashamed? Embarrassed? Sorry?" she offered.

"Yes."

"Good!"

"Good?" I questioned.

"Yep. Feeling bad when you done wrong is good. Tomorrow you go talk to your friend. Tell him how you feel, say you's sorry, ask for forgiveness. Is he your friend?"

"I don't know anymore."

"But was he your friend?" she asked.

"Of course. You know that. The best friend I ever had."

"If he was your friend, he still be your friend. If every mistake ended a friendship, nobody would ever have a friend."

I let her words sunk in. She was almost always right. I believed what she was saying. Or, I just needed to believe.

"Maybe I should go and talk to him now," I suggested.

"Nah. It too soon and too late."

"Too soon and too late?"

"Yep. Too soon after the fight, and too late at night. Let him think. Tomorrow, after both of you have a good sleep and the sun is rising, things will look better. Things always look better in the morning."

She rose from the table and started the ritual of clearing away the dishes. I helped, and when things were cleaned up, I settled in to do my homework. I decided to turn in early. I was still a little lightheaded.

Besides, sleep was a safe place to escape from a bad day.

•••

The next morning I got up early, ate breakfast, gathered my things and hustled out the door. Naani kidded me that maybe I should fight with Tadashi more often, so she wouldn't have to help me get up. I wasn't counting on my wake-up call from Tadi this morning.

I went to the path and waited. He'd have to come

right by me and then I'd make him listen.

I'd decided it wasn't just Tadashi I needed to apologize to, but all the kids, including Toshio. What I did, popping him in the mouth, was okay. What I'd said, popping off my mouth with all that Japanese stuff, was wrong and I'd say so.

I made myself comfortable, slumping against a big rock on the side of the path. The rock blocked the wind and the sun shone down brightly, making it almost warm. I had a book in my backpack, but I thought it was more respectful to just wait in silence. I glanced at my watch. More than twenty minutes had already passed.

I heard voices in the distance. I stood up but then realized they were coming from my village and not from the other direction. It was the little kids, my younger cousins, who always had to leave earlier because they couldn't move as fast. As they passed they offered me hellos and kept on going. Soon I was standing in silence again. The only sound was the wind pulsing through the tree tops.

Before I had a chance to sit down again, others came out of my village. More greetings and invitations to join them were made. I declined. Peter gave me a two-word warning, "No trouble," before he walked off. More trouble was the last thing I wanted. They disappeared down the path toward school and I glanced again at my watch.

I sat down on the sunny rock to wait. Something was wrong. Something was definitely wrong. I strained my eyes down the path and perked my ears to detect anybody coming. Nothing. I'd give them five more minutes. Then, if I ran really hard, I could still get there on time.

I repeatedly looked at my watch. The seconds turned to a minute and then the minute into five. I had to go. My urge was to run up the trail, to Sikima and away from school, to find them. I knew I couldn't do that. Maybe they'd all left early or for some reason taken a boat in, or something. Anyway, I had to get going. I turned and ran.

I caught up to Jonnie and Peter just as they entered the school yard. They were talking. Actually Jonnie was talking a mile a minute, and Peter was listening or pretending to listen. I walked beside them, panting for breath, after running so hard. We entered school and took our seats.

It was instantly apparent that neither Tadashi, nor anybody else from his village, was at school. I looked around. There wasn't a Japanese kid in the class. What was happening? What was this all about? For a second, one weird second, I wondered if the fight yesterday, and the things I'd said, had caused them all to stay away.

Mrs. James tapped the end of a ruler against the blackboard. This was her signal for quiet. We all stopped shuffling and talking and coughing and listened.

"I have some important news, perhaps some of you have already heard it," she started, her voice quivering. "On December seventh, last night, the Japanese attacked Pearl Harbor in Hawaii. Almost simultaneously they also launched an attack on the British and Canadian garrisons in Hong Kong. There was a great loss of life. The United States of America, along with Great Britain and, of course, Canada, have declared a state of war with Japan."

There was a buzz of response as people gasped, muttered to themselves or spoke to their neighbors. She tapped the board again. This time nobody responded. She tapped louder and louder without result.

"Please!" she finally shouted, and the room fell silent. "As you will notice, none of your classmates of Japanese origin are present. Their parents have wisely decided to keep them home today. This is fortunate, as I need the opportunity to speak to the rest of you. Our countries are in a state of war. We must be aware of this.

While I know many of them are your friends, for the good of our Dominion and the British Commonwealth, we must watch and listen and report any suspicious behavior."

A couple of the kids had questions, but I was too stunned to pay attention. What did all this mean? Did she want us to spy on our friends? Did we have reason to worry? I needed to talk to Tadi.

Unfortunately, I'd have to wait longer than just the end of the school day. I had to go to the base right after school. They were having some sort of big get-together. This meant I'd probably be working until late and staying overnight. Usually this suited me just fine. Not tonight.

●●●

"What are you doing up so early?" my mother asked, rubbing sleep out of her eyes.

"I've got to get going," I replied, bending down to tie up my shoelaces.

"To see Tadashi?" she questioned, although it really wasn't a question. She already knew, like she always already knew. "How about some breakfast first?"

"No, I don't want to be late."

"You should eat. Wait until it gets light."

"Don't tell me you think I'll run into forest spirits," I kidded her as I straightened up and got my jacket from the back of one of the kitchen chairs.

"Spirits, no. Other things, yes."

"Other things?"

"A couple of the perimeter guards spotted a cougar last week, and we found bear droppings right in the middle of the parade grounds two days ago."

"Droppings? Are you sure?"

"Come on, Jed," she answered, smiling, "I've seen bear poop a few times in my life. Major Brown tore a strip off all the guards who were on duty that night. He wanted to know how they managed to miss a five-hundred-pound bear."

"Doesn't surprise me," I chuckled, "The way these guys stand guard they could miss a bear … playing a drum … riding a motorcycle."

She came over and gave me a big hug. Instead of letting go after a few seconds, she held on and squeezed extra tight.

"Jed, you be careful. Okay?"

"Don't worry, no bear's going to get me."

"That's not what I mean." She released her grip, slightly, so that she could look me in the face. "Jed, things between you and your friend are probably not ever going to be the same."

"I can make them the same," I protested.

"Sometimes things are so big, we can't control them. Things just happen and we can't make them un-happen," her voice was practically a whisper.

I looked at her closely. What did she know?

She read my eyes. "There are lots of rumors. Sometimes that's all there is around an army camp. Everything is secret, so everybody makes up stories."

"What kind of stories?"

"Lots," she answered. "Most are just crazy, but I don't think it's going to be easy for the Japanese around here, not easy at all."

She pulled me close again for a hug and then released me from her arms. This time I held on just a little bit longer.

"I'll see you later on today. I'll come right back after school."

She nodded in agreement and turned away. Just before she turned, I thought I saw the first hint of tears in the corners of her eyes.

The forest was quiet except for the sounds of my feet crunching the deadfall or breaking through the thin layers of ice that had formed overnight on the tops of puddles. I moved determinedly in a straight line, not around obstacles but right over them. Nothing, no rock or tree or bog was going to stop me this morning. More light was filtering through the trees and I could tell it was going to be a rare December morning, clear and sunny. A good omen.

After a long trek, I came to the rocks overlooking the village. I climbed right over the top; nothing was going to get in my way. At the crest of the outcrop, I could see the village unfold below me. It was beautiful; little neat houses all nestled around the harbor with the ocean visible behind that. It was so quiet.

Quiet. I looked at my watch and saw it was almost seven o'clock. There should have been more activity; kids playing outside, fishermen working on their nets on the dock, something. There was nothing. There wasn't any movement. The only sound was the ocean. Something was terribly wrong.

I felt a wave of fear pass through me. My legs felt all weak and I had to sit down on a rock. I stared down at the houses. Nothing. Then, out of the corner of my eye I caught sight of movement. Two men came out of one of the houses. I recognized the uniforms immediately. They were RCMP officers. They walked down the path of the house and closed the gate behind them. They moved to the next house and knocked on the door. The door opened and they disappeared inside.

Part of me wanted to leave the rocks and get home as soon as possible. Another part wanted me to just sit here and keeping watching. Both were wrong. The right thing to do was to finish what I'd started.

I started down the rock face to the village. I pressed myself close to the rocks, not for fear of falling but of being seen. I imagined unseen eyes peering out of all the windows. I paused at the base of the rocks and slid behind a clump of bushes. I was just getting ready to move forward again when I heard the sound of a door opening. Another pair of RCMP officers were leaving a house. One of them was carrying something. It looked like a radio and a camera, but I couldn't tell for sure from that distance. I heard them talking, and then the one carrying the objects headed towards the dock while the other walked down the front path of the next house. He knocked on the door and was let inside.

Obviously there were more than one pair of officers here in the village. I wondered how many. They'd probably come in by launch, now tied up to the dock. I wasn't sure why, but I didn't want the RCMP to see me. All I was doing was coming to see my friend, but it felt like I was doing something wrong, like I was breaking a law. It didn't matter though, I was going to see Tadashi.

I left the cover of the bushes. Rather than heading straight for his house, I moved off to the side to put a couple of houses between me and the two homes I knew held the RCMP. Passing by the first house, I saw all the blinds were tightly drawn. That was strange. I looked around and realized every window I could see was covered. It was eerie. I felt a sense of dread.

I circled around the house and ran across the dirt road and down a small pathway. I hopped the fence surrounding Tadashi's house and cut across the garden. Hidden behind some shrubs, I stopped, took a deep breath and looked around again. It was still all clear. I walked up to the door and softly knocked. I was taken aback when it opened almost instantly. Tadashi's father stood at the door with his eyes on the ground.

"Hello, Mr. Fukushima," I said quietly.

He looked up and his eyes widened in surprise.

"Can I speak to Tadashi?"

Without answering, he turned away from the door and retreated, leaving the door open. I heard a few words spoken in Japanese and Tadashi rushed to the door.

"What are you doing here?"

"I just wanted to …"

"Get in here, quickly!" he commanded before I could finish answering. He pulled me in by the arm, poked his head out the door, looked all around and then closed the door behind him. The room was thrown into darkness and it took a few seconds for my eyes to adjust. The only light was from a lamp softly glowing in the corner.

"You shouldn't be here."

"I had to talk to you. I had to tell you how sorry I am."

"It isn't your fault."

"It isn't? Who else can I blame for the stupid things I said to Toshio. You know I didn't mean any of that stuff, don't you?"

"Yeah, I know. And you're right they were stupid things, but I'm not thinking about the fight. We have other things to worry about."

"Why are the RCMP here?"

"To check our registration papers and to take away things we shouldn't have."

"Take away things? What sort of things?"

"We're not allowed to have cameras or radio transmitters or maps and charts or guns or weapons of any kind. We have to turn everything over." He motioned to a pile of things in the middle of the table. Included in the pile was my gun.

"My rifle!" I'd loaned it to Tadashi so he could hunt with me at the camp.

Tadashi walked over and picked it up. "Here, better you take it than they do."

"But … but why are they taking any of these things?"

I asked in confusion. I took the gun and cradled it in my arms.

"Because we've been declared Enemy Aliens. They're taking away things we could use to help the enemy ... the Japanese Imperial Army."

"Tadashi!" Mr. Fukushima's stern voice cut through the darkness of the other room.

Tadi disappeared into his parents' room. He returned almost instantly.

"My father said it is necessary for you to leave right away."

I nodded. "Don't worry, the RCMP won't see me."

"It's more than that."

I frowned, confused.

"You shouldn't be here to see all of this. That's why my father is in the other room ... why the shades and blinds are all drawn. Something like this should not be seen."

"I understand," I responded, although I really didn't.

Tadi went over to the front window and lifted the blind ever so slightly so he could look outside.

"It's clear." He moved to the door and opened it a crack.

I hurried over and stopped. "Tadi ... I ..."

"It's all clear ... go!" He pushed me out the door.

I moved quickly down the front path and through the gate. I closed it behind me. I started first in my usual direction, towards home, but stopped, realizing this route led me farther through the village with a greater chance of being seen. The best way was to head completely in the opposite direction to the nearest forest cover. Then I could circle around the village under cover of trees, safe from the eyes of the RCMP. I hurried down the road.

"Heeyyy!"

I stopped dead in my tracks. Slowly, I turned towards

the cry. Two officers moved towards me. They strode briskly in my direction. With alarm I saw them both unbutton their holsters. What were they doing?

"Put down your weapons!" one of them commanded.

What did he mean? What did he want me to …

"Now! Do it now!" the second one barked more urgently.

One officer put a hand on his side arm. My mind snapped back into gear and I bent down, placing my rifle on the ground at my feet. I started to straighten back up.

"The second one too. The one on your back!"

In the rush of the moment I'd forgotten I was carrying a second weapon. I pulled it off my back and laid it down beside the first. Both men seemed to relax and the one removed his hand from his revolver.

"Who are you and what are you doing here?" demanded one.

"I'm Jed Blackburn, and I'm not doing nothing. I'm just taking a shortcut through the village."

"Carrying two rifles?"

"I was out hunting."

"And you figured maybe you might lose your first gun and need a second?"

"I'm just trying out a new rifle and I wanted to make sure I had my regular gun in case the new one didn't work so good." The speed of that lie amazed me.

"Any luck?" asked the second.

I shook my head.

"Bad hunting," he replied.

"Or a bad story," his partner added. "I want to know why an Indian wearing a Canadian army uniform, is walking through a Japanese village, carrying two restricted rifles."

"I'm not an Indian," I objected, "and I can carry any guns I want."

"Don't be giving me lip, boy. Show some respect for the law." He came suddenly forward and scooped up the two rifles. I had to fight the urge to reach out and try to stop him.

"And until such time as you can verify your name, address and your reasons for being here I am taking possession of these weapons."

"You can't do that!"

"I have full authority to take all weapons found within the confines of this village and I am going to follow that authority to the ..."

"Frank," the other officer said quietly, placing a hand on his shoulder. "I want you to give me the guns and proceed to the next house. Leave this matter with me."

Frank hesitated.

"Frank, unless somebody added two stripes to your shoulder when I wasn't looking, I still outrank you. Please move on," the officer directed.

Frank handed over the weapons, turned on his heels and left. We both watched him proceed to the next home, knock on the door and be ushered inside. We turned back to face each other.

"Where do you live, Jed?"

"Down the coast. The next village towards town."

He nodded slowly. "That's a Tsimshian village, isn't it."

"Yeah."

"And you live there, but you're not Tsimshian."

"I live there. My mother is Haida."

"I see. And can you explain to me why you're wearing a Canadian army jacket?"

"It was given to me by the major ... by Major Brown. He runs the camp and my mother is the cook. I do some hunting for them."

He nodded his head again. "Here, take these," he said, handing me both my rifles.

I slung them both onto my shoulder.

"Go home. This isn't a good place for you to be."

"Yes, sir."

"Come, I'll walk you to the edge of the village, so there aren't any more difficulties if you're seen by another officer."

He fell into stride beside me.

"I don't suppose you'd like to explain to me why, if you were going home, you were headed across Sikima away from your village."

I couldn't think of any lie to explain that.

"That's all right. Let's just let it remain one of those little unexplained mysteries."

He stopped as we came to the line where the path emptied out of the forest and into the village.

"And Jed, I have to apologize for my partner. He usually isn't that way. This is a very difficult job and I think we're all on edge. There's not a man in my detachment who thinks this is right."

I think he read my questioning gaze.

"We don't write the laws, only enforce them. Take care."

He walked back into the village and I headed for home.

.13.

Between the rain and the chill in the air, it was a miserable day. Tadashi and I had tramped mile after mile, and hadn't found anything. Heck, I hadn't even caught a glimpse of anything. I told Tadashi that the animals were all too smart to be out in weather like this. It also had to do with Tadashi. He made so much noise when he moved, he could scare away dead animals.

Tadashi wasn't allowed to carry a rifle anymore. This didn't make much of a difference since he hadn't ever managed to hit anything before. He came along to help spot game and we split the money for each kill. He didn't feel comfortable with this arrangement, but this was the only money coming into his home now.

The last two weeks had been hard for the Japanese. They weren't allowed to leave their villages without permission. This meant no school for the kids, work for the men or even trips to Rupert for supplies. Tadashi had permission from the major to be with me anytime I was at the base, but the major warned me to keep Tadashi close at hand and insisted that he only work in the kitchen and not out front serving. There were always new soldiers and visitors around who wouldn't necessarily understand Tadashi being on the base. And of course, people like Stevenson who never did think he should have been there in the first place. At first I was upset about these restrictions, but my mother explained how the major was sticking his neck out, allowing Tadashi there at all.

My rain poncho had kept most of me reasonably dry. There was a line on my pants at the point where the poncho ended, and I was soaked from there down into my boots. My feet were the worst. A couple of times I'd been sucked down into a bog, and with each step I could feel the water slopping around between my toes. All I could think about was dry socks and a big cup of hot coffee.

The camp was still at some distance, but I could hear the sounds of the chain saws reverberating off the trees. I whistled for Tadashi and he turned in my direction. I signaled him to come over. We weren't going to find any game now.

Silently he fell in beside me. The silence didn't surprise me. Not that Tadi would ever talk your ear off, but he hadn't said more than two dozen words all day.

"Not a good day," I said trying to start up a conversation.

"Nope. Seen better."

"How's your family doing?" I hadn't been to his village since the same morning the RCMP were there. Tadashi hadn't invited me and I didn't feel right going there without an invitation right now.

"Okay I guess … different for different people."

This held promise of an actual conversation. "What do you mean?"

"My father doesn't want to talk about it. He leaves the house every morning like he's going off to fish. He goes down to the storage sheds and works on refitting the boat and fixing the nets."

"I guess that's pretty smart, getting ready for next year's fishing season."

"But the boat was already put away, ready for next year and the nets didn't have any holes anyway," Tadashi explained.

"I guess it's hard for him to just sit around. And your grandmother?"

"Even stranger. She seems almost content. She keeps muttering 'shikata-ga-nai,' which means 'it can't be helped.' She says things could be worse, and at least we're together. That's how all the *Issei*, the older people, are acting. It's no wonder the whites can't understand the Japanese, I can hardly understand them myself."

"It'll change," I offered. "They can't make you stay in the village forever."

"Nope, that's for sure. Course I've heard rumors they might make us leave our homes."

"Come on, Tadi, you can't believe everything you hear. They can't make you leave your homes. This is Canada … a democracy. That's just crazy talk."

"Maybe … but is it any crazier than what's already happened?"

I wanted to answer, to reassure him everything would be okay, that everything would go back to the way it was, but I couldn't.

Just ahead we were coming up to the first teams of men from the camp. They were in pairs wielding gigantic two-man chain saws. This was dangerous and dirty work. Surrounding them was a cloud of sawdust filling the air, coating the men, the machine and the ground with a thick layer. The men were firmly anchored in the ground, almost buried up to their knees in mud. The mud was everywhere. Over the past few days other crews had taken away all the underbrush and now the rain, which hadn't let up for what seemed like forever, had turned the ground into a quagmire.

I couldn't help but smile when I looked at the first two guys, joined together at the chain saws. They were completely covered with grime and mud and sawdust and sap and sweat and oil. The oil was from the chain saws. They had to spray it on the blade as a lubricant and it flew off as they worked the saw back and forth. The oil was like the glue holding everything else in place. Filthy didn't even come close to describing them.

I could see them opening their mouths, yelling at each other, but couldn't hear anything over the roar of the saw. Then, the sound of the chain saws drifted off, chortled and echoed away to nothing. One of the guys yelled out his message and then, realizing he was no longer competing with the saw, lowered his voice to a near normal level. At that very moment they noticed us. It was funny but it seemed like the roar of the chain saws hadn't just masked their hearing but had put blinders on their sight. Now that it was quiet they could see again.

"Hey, guys, any luck today?" asked one. His name was Patterson. He was a friend of Smitty's. Friendly, but quiet.

"No luck," I said. "Just hope we didn't catch pneumonia."

"Too nice a day to die," Patterson answered.

"Nice day?" Tadashi asked.

"Not yet, my young friend, but it will be," he winked at his partner.

"That's right," added his friend, a guy named Varga. "There's still time for this to become a great day." I didn't know Varga too well; he'd been assigned to the camp only a few weeks before. I looked at them both, wondering if they were insane. Maybe the chain saw had vibrated their brains a little too hard.

"Tonight's the night," Patterson continued. "Big dance down in Rupert."

"Dance?" I said.

"You know, putting your arms around a lady and moving to the music."

"Ah, ladies," Varga sighed, "wonderful, delightful ladies."

"The local Red Cross has arranged for a delegation to come up from Vancouver. I heard the band is an all-female orchestra," Patterson added.

"Enough, enough already, a female orchestra," Varga groaned. "We gotta get outa here. Isn't it time for us to call it a day?"

Patterson looked at his wrist and then realized all he wore was a thick layer of mud. "Forgot I'd taken it off. If you wear a watch while you're using one of these things, it just vibrates the heck out of it. Jed, you got the time?"

"It's almost five," I replied.

"Five o'clock!" Varga yelled. "Let's get back to the base. We have to get cleaned up, fed, dressed and into town!"

They both worked to pull themselves away from the grip of the mud. There was a terrible sucking sound as their legs pulled free.

"Damn!" yelled Patterson.

"What's wrong?" Varga questioned.

"My boot," he moaned. "My boot. I've lost it down there." Patterson pointed down to the sea of mud, then held up his left foot which was covered by only a muddy sock. Varga started to laugh and I couldn't keep a smile off my face.

"This isn't funny. Help me look." Patterson stood on one foot, balancing like a muddy flamingo.

"Help?" Varga answered. "No way I'm sticking my arm into that mud. Might come up short a finger or two. We don't have time for this. Come on, let's get going."

"Get going? How am I going to get going without my boot?"

"Mike, how much dirtier can you get anyway? I'll carry the saw and you hop back to camp."

Tadashi pulled his empty game bag off his shoulder. "Here, put your foot inside this."

"But what about my boot?"

· 149 ·

"It's history, forget it," Varga advised. "You told me they once lost a jeep in this mud, so I don't think there's much chance of finding your boot. Consider it a casualty of war."

"But my boot ..." Patterson muttered again.

"Your choice. Spend the night here in the dark, in the rain, in the mud, looking for a stinking old work boot, or, come to the dance ... clean clothes, drinks, good food, soft music and ... wonderful women. You remember women, don't you, Mike? They're a lot like men except not as hairy, they smell better and ..."

Patterson hopped over and took the game bag. "Thanks." He put his foot inside and then wrapped it around so it would stay in place.

The four of us made our way towards the camp. Each group of men we passed stopped working and joined in with us. Soon Tadashi and I were in a small mob of happy men. All the conversation was about the dance. I never figured these guys liked dancing so much.

By the time we reached camp, there must have been fifty guys trailing behind us. Fifty truly filthy guys, covered in the remains of their work efforts. Walking at the front of this pack, all I needed was a flute to make me look like the pied piper of dirt.

There was another cluster of men who'd already beaten us to camp. They were standing around by the showers. They looked identical to the group I was with. Getting closer though, I could tell there was one big difference; they weren't happy. They were angry. There was pushing and shoving and swearing.

Varga was one of the first to meet the crowd. "What's going on here? What's the hold up?"

Different people mumbled different answers, and then Murdock stepped out of the crowd. "I'll tell you what's happening," he thundered. "It's those damn officers! Not one of them has been working a spit all day and now they're taking the showers. Been in there, using up all the hot water. We pounded on the door and they told us to leave or else!"

Murdock had been busted down from an MP and a sergeant to a lowly corporal when the major found him in the bootleg business. Major Brown had got suspicious when every week Murdock's mail contained a dozen loaves of bread. The major had a loaf broken open, "by accident," and found a mickey of booze buried away in the middle.

This was how Murdock was getting his supply. His brother back in Toronto bought a bottle for two bucks, stuffed it in a loaf of bread for safekeeping and mailed it to Murdock, who sold it for twenty-five dollars. After he found that first bottle of booze, the major had sent for both Murdock and George Star. The rest of the loaves were broken open in front of them. George got to see the major keep his word, and Murdock got to see his liquor and his stripes being washed down the drain.

Since then, Murdock had been even meaner than before. Even more than the loss of money or rank, I figured he just missed the chance to beat up on people. Not that he still didn't do that whenever an officer wasn't around, but he just couldn't do it as often. He was like a dark storm cloud, hovering over the base, causing trouble of one sort or another.

"What right do these officers have to take all the hot water," Murdock roared. "The way we're covered with filth, we're the ones who need the hot water to have any chance of getting clean."

The crowd of men had gotten pretty quiet, listening to him.

"Do any of you jokers think you have a chance of getting close to a lady tonight if you can't get close to some hot water and soap first?"

Now the quiet was broken as men started to yell in

agreement or mumble or talk to themselves. A voice, I don't know whose voice, broke through. "What can we do?"

Murdock jumped up on top of a large rock, which put him head and shoulders above the crowd. He didn't answer right away and I knew he was thinking — or more likely — plotting. His expression was still angry but his eyes looked empty. A slight smile came to his face and became a nasty smirk.

"We'll show them," he said, quietly at first. "We'll show them!" This time his voice was as loud as thunder. "Follow me!"

I felt a wave of fear flow up my spine. I didn't know what he was going to do, but I knew I wouldn't like it. The men trailed after him, cheering him on. Somebody had to stop them. But who? Major Brown would already be down in Rupert. He and George Star had become friends and spent each Saturday night together in a jeep riding up and down the main street. All the MPs would already be gone as well. Smitty! They'd listen to Smitty.

"Tadi, get Smitty ... fast!" I yelled. Tadashi ran down the incline towards the motor pool.

The mob stopped around Eddy. Eddy! What did they want with Eddy? With the heavy rain today he'd be sitting safely inside sheltered from the weather. We'd recently put him on a longer tether, almost twenty feet long, because with all the test flights he was making from the top of his little house, we were afraid he'd strangle himself. He now spent hours gliding down the few feet from roof top to ground.

I raced forward until I was stopped by the backs of the group of tightly bunched men. I screamed out, but my voice was lost in the yelling and hollering. I watched helplessly as Murdock and two other guys pushed a piece of plywood over the entrance to the house, trapping Eddy inside. Then one man held the board in place while six or seven others bent down and picked the entire house up. The rope, one end of it on one of Eddy's legs and the other end attached to the house, dragged behind. It could get tangled up in all the feet and Eddy would get slammed against the wood or have his leg pulled off. To my relief somebody gathered up the loops of rope and carried it along with the house.

This made no sense. What were they going to do to Eddy? I shoved and scrambled through until I stood directly in front of the men carrying the house. They came striding towards me with Murdock in the lead. I positioned myself so I was right in his path. Murdock saw me and a scowl came to his face. His eyes filled with a look that was a cross between anger and happiness.

"Get out of the way, injun!" he yelled.

I was hit by a wave of fear, but wasn't getting out of anybody's way. I planted my feet in the mud.

"Move!" he yelled, and then with one motion, he swept out his arm. It hit me across the side of my head and I went sprawling, flying through the air. I bounced into the legs of a couple of soldiers and then landed in the mud. I looked up to see the dog house move away. Patterson helped me to my feet. Most of the soldiers were no longer following. They stood like stony, silent statues, watching. The sound, the rumblings of the mob, was also gone. All I could hear was Murdock swearing, and the voices of his friends carrying the house, hurling out encouragement.

Murdock ran slightly up ahead of the others and flung open the door, the only door, to the showers. A cloud of steam rose from the opening and into the sky. The opening to Eddy's house, still covered by the plywood, was pushed up against the opened door of the showers. Murdock then jumped on top of the house and pulled up the plywood. Two of the others started kicking the back of it. I caught a glimpse of a wing tip before it vanished into the steam-filled air of the showers.

The shower building had eight showers separated by low partitions. It wasn't very large, slightly longer, and definitely narrower, than the tether line on Eddy's foot.

The only sound now was the steady plopping of the rainwater in the puddles and the background rumble of the showers. All eyes were trained on that small door, the bottom part blocked by the house. It felt like everybody was holding their breath, waiting.

Then there was the screech of Eddy screaming out a threat. Almost immediately, it was followed by a series of yells and hollers echoing out of the showers as the officers become aware, probably all at once, that they were sharing their shower.

Eddy was a lot friendlier than when he first came to the camp. When he was in a good mood — Naani had helped me to figure out how to read his moods — he'd gently take a mouse or a piece of meat right out of my fingers. But now, soaking wet, in a new place with everybody yelling and running around, and probably pretty frightened, Eddy would not be in a good mood.

Through the haze of steam rising out of the door, a figure came hurtling over the house. One of the officers, naked and temporarily clean, cleared the house with just the touch of one hand on the top. He landed, skidded and then slid face first into the mud. Before he even finished his slide, a second and third man followed. Both landed almost exactly in the tracks of the first, and the three crashed together at the end into a muddy ball of arms and legs.

"How many men are in there?" I asked Patterson.

"Don't know, but I think all of the officers, maybe eight or ten."

Before his sentence had been completed, a fourth man hurtled over the house. He did it cleanly without even touching the roof. I caught a glimpse of red on his side. Eddy had got him! The first three men had got to their feet but were all bowled over by this last man.

"That's a strike!" somebody yelled out, and the crowd, which had been strangely quiet, erupted into laughter.

The four officers, naked, wet, covered with mud, panting and bruised, staggered to their feet again. Two of them moved ahead and tried to shoulder the house away from the entrance to the shower. Their feet slipped and one fell down again, face first, flat in the mud. He pulled himself up. For the first time I looked at one of their faces. It was Stevenson. It looked good on him. He stood up and grabbed the edge of the house where it was against the shower building. He took one of his muddy feet and pushed it against the structure, using it as an anchor. You could almost feel the strain, and then with a "Pop," the house moved away and off to one side. All four of the officers pushed it out of the way, completely clearing the shower door. Stevenson bounded the few steps back to the door and hollered in. I couldn't make out his words, but they generated instant action. Five other men burst out through the opening and rocketed across the open ground.

Out of the mist came Eddy. As he stepped clear, he stopped. He opened his wings fully, threw back his head and screeched, a cry of victory. He gave two little hops and then, his wings flapping, leaped to the top of his house. He balanced, teetering slightly back and forth, flapping his wings, until he was sure of his footing.

Out of the corner of my eye I caught a glimpse of somebody moving along the boardwalk. It was Major Brown! George Star was with him. I didn't know why they were back, but I didn't care. I was just so grateful to see them.

The major stopped at the most elevated part of the

walkway, leaned against the railing and stared out at the mass of filthy men, some standing naked, and all dripping mud. A few others saw him and turned in his direction. The major's mouth opened, and then closed. Then opened and closed again without a syllable emerging. George Star stood just behind his left shoulder.

"Attention!" yelled a voice from the crowd.

The crowd swung around as one to face the voice and then froze into position. Major Brown stared at the men for what was only a few seconds but felt like forever. "Could my officers please put on clothes and assemble in the mess hall. All others are restricted to their barracks. Dismissed!"

I could hear some quiet muttering, but nobody was fool enough to voice any objections. His directions were heeded. The major turned around and both he and George went to the mess.

I scanned the crowd for Tadashi. He was nowhere to be seen. I headed around the side of the mess hall to come in through the kitchen. Rounding the corner I found my mother, mixing bowl in hand, standing and looking out the window of the door. She moved aside so I could enter.

"Did you see it all?" I asked.

"Just the end. Poor old bird … so glad your Naani wasn't here to see any of it." She stopped and her face took on a confused expression. "Come over here," she ordered as she walked to the sink. Obediently I followed behind. She took a cloth, wet it, and started to rub my face.

"Ooouch!"

"You got yourself a nasty bruise and bump coming up on your face. Couldn't see it for a second under all that mud." She moved over to the ice box and removed a piece of ice. She wrapped it in a cloth. "Hold this against your face, it'll take some of the swelling down," she said as she pressed it against my cheek.

"That hurts!" I answered, flinching under its touch.

"What happened?"

"Nothing."

"This isn't a nothing. Don't lie to me, Jedidiah. Never you mind; I'll ask Tadashi."

"He didn't see it," I answered.

"Hah! If nothing happened, how could you know whether he saw it or not?"

"I ... just ..."

"If you don't want to talk about it, or if you're afraid to tell me because I may do something about it, then I'll let you decide what needs to be done. Okay?" she said softly.

I nodded. I didn't like keeping things from her.

"Did this happen because you were trying to protect Eddy?"

Again I nodded.

Her eyes were filled with a look of anger I'd seldom seen before. She reached her hand to the side of my face and pressed the ice pack gently against my cheek.

"I'm gonna stay here with you right now, because if I don't, and I find out who's responsible for this, I'll kill 'em."

"Mom it's okay ... honestly."

"No, it isn't. You just won't know how it feels to have your child hurt until you have one of your own."

We were interrupted by the sound of the front door opening and feet plodding across the floor boards.

"Are you sure you're okay?"

"It's just a little bruise ... I'm fine. Shouldn't we get back to work?"

"Work?"

"Yeah, setting things up out there," I motioned to the dining hall. "I want to know what's going to happen."

She nodded. "Most of the stuff is already in there, so just spread it around and try to look busy while you're eavesdropping." She handed me a big pot of something, and a little bit of steam escaped from the lid which was slightly ajar. "Be careful, hot soup. Make sure you just hold it by the handles."

She gathered up two large trays of potatoes, stacking one on top of the other. We pushed through the swinging door and into the serving area. Major Brown was standing in front of his officers, who had hurriedly dressed but still had patches of mud on their faces or in their hair. George was standing at the far window, looking out, ignoring the scene going on behind him.

"All right, could somebody — perhaps you, Captain Stevenson — explain why all my officers were standing around, without their uniforms, covered with mud," Major Brown began.

"Well, we were trying to get away from the eagle," Stevenson answered firmly. "They brought the eagle over and tossed it into the showers. Those men should be court marshaled! One of us could have been badly hurt or even killed."

"Is anyone hurt?" Major Brown asked.

One of them raised his hand, half-heartedly, like he was embarrassed.

"Yes, Lieutenant Hicks?"

"I got cut up because of that eagle," he answered.

"Where is your injury?"

"Lieutenant Hicks pulled up his shirt and showed his arm.

"The eagle did that?"

"Not exactly, sir," Lieutenant Hicks replied.

"Well, how exactly did it happen?"

"When we spotted the eagle there was a bit of a scramble, and somebody bumped against me and I hit into the soap holder."

"So, you are telling me that you were wounded by a soap holder!" Major Brown shook his head. "Congratulations, Lieutenant, you are the first man in the history of the Canadian army, perhaps in the history of any army, to be wounded in that manner. I'll cable away for your Purple Heart immediately."

Stevenson spoke up. "That wouldn't have happened if they hadn't thrown in that damn bird. Its beak and claws are like razors. We're lucky none of us lost anything in there! Those men have to be punished."

"Yes, and they will, but first I have to know why. Can you explain why all my officers, who have been working indoors all day, were taking showers while all the enlisted men, who were working outdoors, were waiting in the mud and rain?"

Nobody wanted to answer that question.

"Does anybody think there might be a connection between these two events?" he asked. "Now, can someone tell me who I should punish? Who is responsible?"

"Whoever carried that eagle house over to the showers," Stevenson answered.

"And who is that?"

"I'm not sure. We could just punish everybody," Stevenson continued. "Cancel all leaves, keep everybody confined to their barracks."

"And why are you not sure of who specifically we should punish?"

"Well ... we don't really know because ... we were all in the showers ..."

"Leaving who in charge?" Major Brown demanded.

"Well ... I guess still me, even if I was in the showers."

"Wrong answer, Captain Stevenson, and worse still, wrong attitude. You left this camp without command, so there is no one who can tell me what happened!" Major Brown yelled. "One of you get me Murdock. Either he caused this or he'll tell me who did. The rest of you go to your posts and await my further orders."

Stevenson looked like he was going to speak back.

He wasn't smart enough to stop his mouth from opening, but wasn't stupid enough to actually say anything. They filed out of the mess hall. With the closing of the door, George motioned for the Captain to come to the window.

"What ya going to do with that eagle, Bob?"

"I don't know. I haven't had any time to think about the bird. I've got other things to take care of."

"Let Jed and his friend out there take care of it, okay?" George requested.

"What ever ... I mean, thank you, I would appreciate that."

"Jed, quit pretending you're working and go on outside and watch the eagle. Don't get too close. Have to let it calm down some before you try to move it back."

I went out the door and found Tadashi sitting on the edge of the boardwalk, close by Eddy. Except for the two of them, there wasn't another living soul in sight. The rest of the base was completely deserted as every single man was in his barracks.

"Are you okay?" Tadashi asked.

"Mostly."

"I saw what he did to you ... I couldn't believe it."

"I'm okay, really. Old Toshio hurt me worse than this," I reassured him.

"And Eddy ... nobody has a right to do that ... bad enough he's tied up, but to be humiliated like that ..."

"He looks like he's okay."

"Maybe he's not injured, but what about his spirit?" Tadashi asked.

"You sound like my Naani."

"Maybe because she's right! You can't just chain up a creature like that, take away its freedom and dignity and stop it from going where it belongs and ..." He stopped and rose to his feet. "And do you know the worst part, Jed? If they hadn't stopped me from carrying a gun … if I had a rifle with me … I would have shot Murdock."

I put a hand on the strap of my rifle and looked up into Tadashi's eyes.

I knew he was telling the truth.

The vet asked, "How's its appetite. Is it eating okay?"

"I guess so," I answered, "but it's like I said, he's getting more particular. If I can't get him rabbit, and if it isn't a fresh kill, he won't eat it."

"He used to like it cooked in a stew," Tadashi said playfully, kidding me about my Naani's insistence that Eddy was my grandfather. Of course, neither of us took her seriously, but we both had spent a number of evenings sitting off to the side and listening to her tell Eddy his old Haida stories. The stories were interesting, although the most interesting part was how calm Eddy got. He just sat there, his head cocked to one side, not moving.

"Cooked in a stew?" the vet asked.

"Nothing, he's just joking around."

"Joking … I see. It's good he's eating. He's certainly gained weight since the first time I saw him. I just wish he'd eat the mouse, so I could examine him."

The vet had once again stuffed some sleeping capsules in a mouse and given it to Eddy. This time rather than eat it, Eddy just ignored the bait.

"And it would be better if he was on a longer tether so I could see him move more."

"He was," Tadashi answered. There was an edge of bitterness in his voice.

"Was?"

"Yeah. They had to shorten his line because he was

jumping out at people when they came too close."

"Was he flying at them or running?" the vet inquired.

"Sort of running ... with his wings open, I guess. Is that bad?"

"Not good. Does he flap his wings a lot, like he's exercising them?"

"Yeah, he does that!" I answered enthusiastically. "Sometimes he beats them so hard you can feel the breeze."

"But he doesn't do it as much as he used to," Tadashi added.

The vet gave a questioning look and I knew I had to explain things more.

"There was this problem with Eddy last week."

"But it wasn't Eddy's fault or anything," Tadashi said, defending him.

"Yeah, it wasn't his fault. It's just ... he got tossed around by some of the men and ended up in the showers and ..."

"That's cruel! I hope those involved were severely punished!"

They were," I answered, and Tadi and I exchanged a smile.

Murdock was shipped out of camp a few days after the incident. He would have left sooner, but they had to wait for his injuries to heal a bit. I wasn't there, but I heard all about it afterwards. Patterson had told him to pick on somebody more his own size, and Murdock said Patterson was closer to his size and took a swing at him. It ended with Murdock lying in a pool of his own blood with a busted nose and a fractured jaw. I was shocked; Patterson was so quiet. But my mother said she always knew there was strength there. Needless to say, Patterson could always come into the kitchen any time he wanted for an extra portion of meat or a bigger piece of pie.

"Do you think he could have re-injured his wing?"

"I don't know," I said quietly, although that was my

fear all along. "Maybe I can go out and get a rabbit and you can put some more pills inside and …"

"I don't have time for that," the vet interrupted. "Besides, there's a limit to what I can tell in an examination. I think the wing is as good as it's going to get. Only way to really tell is to see him fly."

"You mean we're going to release him?" I asked.

"We can try … I just don't know if it's the best thing."

"Why wouldn't it be the best thing?" Tadashi asked.

"From what you two have said, I'm sure it can fly, at least a little. But I'm doubtful that it can fly well enough to survive."

Tadashi frowned. "I don't understand."

"For an eagle to survive in the wild it has to be in perfect shape. If there are any problems, it won't be able to catch food and it'll get weaker and weaker … a slow and painful death."

"But maybe he can," I argued.

"Maybe. But are you prepared to take a gamble like that?"

"What other choice is there?" I asked. "He can't stay here forever."

"I was speaking to the major about one other option. I have a colleague who works for the zoo down in Vancouver and they recently lost one of the bald eagles in their exhibit …"

"You want to put Eddy in a zoo?" I asked in disbelief.

"We'd be assured the eagle would be all right. He'd be well fed and cared for. Research even shows that zoo animals live longer than those in the wild."

"That's no way to live, all caged up," Tadashi said.

"It's better to live that way than not live at all," the vet countered.

"Shows how much you know," Tadi muttered under his breath and then turned and walked away. I started after him.

"Jed!"

I turned around. It was the major, walking toward Eddy and the vet. Good, I needed to talk to him about Eddy going to a zoo. I arrived in time to hear the end of their conversation.

"... if you can report to my office after you've finished your examination, I would appreciate it," the major said. He turned to me and he had a deadly serious look on his face. "Jed, we need to talk. Please come with me." The major started walking back towards the mess. I fell into step beside him.

I got a sinking feeling in my stomach. I knew what he wanted to say: Eddy was going to the zoo. My mind was filled with a rush of feelings and thoughts. It wasn't fair! He couldn't just send Eddy away without even discussing it with me. After all it was me who was feeding the eagle and watching out for him and putting out fresh water and ...

"Jed, I have something important to tell you."

"Yeah, I know."

"You do?" he questioned.

"Yeah, the vet told us already."

"The vet? How would the vet know?"

"He told us somebody he knew at the zoo would take Eddy," I answered, suddenly confused by the question.

"Oh ... the eagle. Yes, the vet has mentioned the zoo as a possibility, and I will seriously consider his opinion, but this isn't about the bird. It's about Tadashi."

"Tadashi?" Suddenly the sinking feeling got worse.

"I'm sorry to have to tell you this ... he'll have to leave the base ... he can't be here any more."

"But ..." I wanted to ask why, but of course I already knew.

"I wanted you to know before I told your friend ... I know how close you two are, and I thought it would be good for you to be there to offer him support. A complaint was filed with the area Commander, and I've received orders to discharge him. I have no choice, Jed."

"But you're in charge …"

"I'm in charge here. We all have somebody we have to answer to … I am truly sorry, believe me."

Suddenly Eddy didn't seem so important.

"Jed, why don't you go in and see your mother. I've already discussed it with her and maybe you can talk to her while I inform Tadashi."

"No, you can't."

"I know this is difficult, Jed, but it must be done."

"I know, sir … it's just you can't tell him. He's my friend and he's here because of me … it's me who should talk to him."

The major looked me squarely in the eyes and nodded his head slowly. "Are you sure you want to do this?"

"I know I don't want to, but I'm the one who should."

He put a hand on my shoulder and the look on his face confirmed I was doing the right thing.

"Can I tell him at the end of the day?"

The major shook his head. "He has to be off the base almost right away. A meeting is being held here this morning to coordinate all services. The area commander is chairing the meeting. It has to happen now."

•••

"Well? Is Eddy going to go to the zoo?" Tadashi asked.

"We didn't talk much about him."

He gave me a questioning look. "Funny, from your expression it looks like he told you to come over and shoot Eddy."

"It isn't about Eddy." I paused. "It's about …"

"Me," Tadashi said softly.

"Yeah."

"I can't work here anymore."

"How did you know?" I questioned.

"I knew it was only a matter of time."

"I'm sorry, Tadi. I'm so sorry."

"I know, but there's nothing anybody could do about it. I almost feel relieved."

"How can you feel relieved?"

Tadashi shrugged. "Well, you know, it's like when you're standing there waiting for the principal to hit your palm with the strap. You know it's coming and the waiting is the worst part."

"How would you know about that? You've never got the strap before."

"A friend of mine has and he told me about it … didn't he, Jed," he answered and a smile creased his face.

"Yeah, I guess I have mentioned it before," I admitted. "But you seem so calm about it."

"How else should I feel?"

"I don't know. Sad or upset or maybe angry. I know I feel angry … so angry I feel like … like … quitting!"

"Not working at the base?" he asked.

"Yeah!" I answered, but instantly I wished I'd never said it. I was mad, but the last thing I wanted to do was not be here with my mother.

"Don't go and do anything stupid!" Tadashi protested.

I felt a wave of relief wash over me which I tried to keep off my face.

"Your quitting would only make it worse. Promise me you won't do anything like that, okay?"

I nodded in agreement. "Okay, I guess."

Then I chuckled softly.

"What's so funny?" Tadashi asked.

"I was just thinking about how the major told me so I could give you support. It seems like it's the other way around."

"Yeah, things work out strange sometimes. What did the major say about Eddy?"

"Not much, really. He's listened to the vet, but he

hasn't made a decision yet. I'll talk to him later. It's just there are so many other things happening, it doesn't seem that important."

"That's where you're wrong, Jed. It is important. No matter what happens, you gotta make sure they don't make Eddy live in a zoo. Nothing should have to live locked up like that. Nothing."

.15.

I munched on a sandwich and watched Eddy tear strips off his lunch — a rabbit I'd picked off walking to school yesterday. It wasn't a fresh kill, but it was fresh enough for him to choose to eat it. I wanted to make sure I gave Eddy something big to eat before I left with my mother for her four days off. The new cook didn't seem to be interested in Eddy. She said feeding two hundred soldiers was more than enough to keep her busy.

I still felt angry about Tadashi being gone, angry at the major. My mother explained it all to me, how Major Brown couldn't allow somebody designated as an Enemy Alien to be on the base. She said almost the same thing that RCMP officer had said to me about how he had to follow orders whether he agreed with them or not.

"Jed! Jed!"

I looked up to see Smitty running up the path. He was all arms and legs and ran like a cartoon character.

"Jed, have you heard?"

"Heard what?"

"The Japanese have been ordered to leave Rupert."

"Leave Rupert! That can't be true!"

"Remember who you're talking to," he replied with a hint of indignation.

"Where are they going?" I choked. "When do they have to leave?"

"Don't know where, but I know when. Tomorrow morning."

"That can't be right."

"It is. Got it straight from the horse's mouth. I was just down in Rupert and speaking to a couple of the RCMP. They had to go and give the orders this morning and will be back tomorrow to enforce it."

I tossed the remaining bites of my sandwich to Eddy. He ignored it.

"Could you tell my mom I won't be able to help her anymore today? I gotta go."

"Me?" Smitty said. "Why don't you tell her?"

"Because."

"Because?"

"Just because," I answered.

"More likely because she might not want you to go to the village, so you figure it's better to ask for her forgiveness later than her permission now. Right?"

"Right. Will you tell her?"

He nodded his head. "How much of a head start you want?"

"Ten minutes or so. I don't figure she'll be coming after me."

I had to fight the urge to start running. It was too far to run. Maybe Smitty was wrong. There were always lots of rumors and almost all of them were just talk. I knew Smitty too well to believe he was wrong, but I needed something to keep me going.

•••

Breaking through the trees, I was unprepared for what I saw. Everyone in the whole village seemed to be out on the streets. Old, young, mothers holding their babies, whole families, carrying things and moving towards the harbor. In the harbor, some at anchor rising and falling with the waves, and others tied to the dock, were the fishing boats of the village. The boats which had been put away for the winter were all back in the water.

People were moving, faces blank, eyes flat and focused on the ground. I mumbled greetings which were left unanswered. I felt a wave of panic sweep over me and my stomach clenched tightly into a fist.

I bumped into an old woman. " I'm sorry," I mumbled. I knew her from my visits to the village, but didn't know her name. She looked up at me and her eyes flashed with annoyance. Then those same eyes shifted down to the ground, and she hurried off.

I raced across the village to Tadashi's house. The front door was closed and I pounded on it. Silence. I knocked again. No answer. I stared at the door, hoping to see somehow right through the wood and into the house.

"Hello, Jedidiah," came a familiar voice from behind me.

I spun around quickly. It was Tadashi's grandmother.

"Family all at boat. Be back soon. Come inside," she invited. She opened the front door and I followed behind her. She closed the door and I felt a swelling of safety. In here, things seemed the same.

"Tea?"

"Yeah, I mean, yes please."

"I put on kettle."

"Please, could you explain things to me," I pleaded.

"I don't understand either," she said, shaking her head. "RCMP come, first light, tell us leave by tomorrow."

She was interrupted by the sounds of the front door opening. Tadashi and his father came through the door. They looked shocked, and stopped. In behind them came Yuri and Midori. Midori brushed the hair away from her face and flashed a shy smile.

"Jed!" Yuri blurted. "Have you come to help us move?"

"I came ..." my head was spinning, my stomach churning, ... "I came to say ... I don't know ... just to say goodbye."

Mr. Fukushima nodded an acknowledgment.

"Where are you going to?" I asked.

"We don't know," Tadashi said. "They didn't tell us. Just ordered us to be on our boats and ready to go."

"Is there anything I can do? Can I help you move things?"

Tadashi shook his head. "No need. We're not taking much. There isn't much space. Besides, we hope to be back in our homes soon."

"What can I do?"

"Nothing. I have to go back to the boat," Tadashi said. He turned and walked back through the door.

"Tadi!" I called out, running after him. I grabbed him by the shoulders and spun him around to face me. "I don't know what to say."

"There's nothing to say," he answered. "You have to go. Some of the people in the village are angry. I don't think they'd do anything, but I'm not sure. I've got to get back to loading. Please go ... now."

My hands melted off of his shoulders. He turned and walked away. I stood, stunned, my mouth hanging open, and watched him move away, not looking back.

I felt a tear force its way out and roll down my cheek. My hand went up to wipe it away. Then, without think-ing, on the way back down to my side, it stopped on the top button of my army jacket. The jacket of the army that was forcing my friend to leave. I undid that button. And then the next, and the next, and the last. A shiver ran through my entire body and the jacket slipped off my shoulders and fell to the ground. I stepped back-wards, over the clump of clothes I'd just shed. I looked down. It looked strange just lying on the ground. I knew I couldn't hold back the tears any longer. I sprinted off to the safety of the rocks, running blindly amongst the people moving towards the docks.

I scrambled up the rocks, not stopping until I reached the top. I sat down, curled up my legs, put my head down between my knees and sobbed.

•••

"Here, take this, it's cold." It was Tadashi.

I looked up. He stood overtop of me, my jacket in his outstretched hand. I wiped my face to try to remove the tears.

"Take it," he repeated. "This isn't like Victoria. It's too cold to be out here in January without a jacket."

I didn't move. He took it and draped it over my shoulders.

"Nice jacket." Tadashi sat down on the rocks beside me. "I was so jealous when you got it, and so happy when I got one of my own. The worst part of leaving the base was having to give mine back. I was the only Japanese in all of Canada wearing one of those. Pretty special, eh?"

I pulled the jacket tightly around me but couldn't think of anything to say.

"I spent last night crying," he said.

I nodded. "I'm sorry, Tadi, I'm sorry for everything," I said quietly.

"So am I."

We sat, side by side, without talking, staring at the scene played out below us.

"Tadi … I'm glad you came up here."

"You should be. You would have frozen without your jacket."

"You know what I mean."

He stood up, then offered me his hand and pulled me to my feet.

"I've got to go," he said. He still held my hand. "Take

care, Jed, take care."

"You too, Tadi."

He turned and took a few steps.

"Wait!" I called out. He stopped.

I stood up and walked to his side. "We have one more thing to do before you have to leave," I said.

.16.

"You don't need to turn the flashlight off yet," I said. "We're still pretty far from the base."

"I didn't turn it off. It just stopped working." Tadashi shook the light and smacked it with the palm of his hand, but it didn't start up again.

"Here, let me give it a try." I took the flashlight from his hands and fiddled with it. It didn't spark to life, so I gave it a hard slap with the side of my hand.

"Gee, why didn't I think of that?" he asked sarcastically. "Besides, it might be better without the light. There's less chance of us being seen by one of the patrols if we move in the dark. You can get us to the camp without the light?"

"'Course I can. I always said I could find the way with my eyes closed. Just stay right behind me and try to walk quietly." I guessed we'd find out if I was right.

It was a clear night. The half moon peeked through the openings between the trees and thousands of pin-pricks of stars, scattered like somebody had tossed up a handful of salt into the sky, punctuated the night. When Tadashi and I met on the big rock along the path between our villages, I'd prayed for the sky to become overcast to offer us better protection from prying eyes. Now without the flashlight, I was thankful for the trickles of light from the sky.

"Be careful," I whispered. "Trip wires up ahead …

step over them carefully."

We both gingerly stepped over the wires. This marked the farthest line of the camp defenses. From this point on we'd have to be on the lookout for patrols. There could be anywhere from three to four pairs of men walking the perimeter.

I pricked up my ears. I knew we'd hear them before we could see them. It was almost impossible to move quietly wearing army boots. I was grateful for moccasins. I wore my old comfortable pair while Tadashi was wearing a pair of my Naani's which I'd borrowed for the evening. I didn't expect her to be out walking at three in the morning, so I figured she wouldn't be needing them the rest of the night.

There were patches of snow on the ground but mainly it was bare. The earth was frozen, and, despite the moccasins, occasionally we'd step on a patch of ice and it would crack underneath noisily. It was cold and I felt a chill throughout my body. That was partly fear, but it was also partly due to the fact that I was wearing my peacoat, which wasn't nearly as thick as my army jacket. I just thought it wasn't right to wear it tonight. Not right because I was sneaking into the base and somehow it seemed disrespectful. And not right because Tadashi was with me.

Up ahead I heard sounds. We both froze. I crouched down and motioned for Tadashi to do the same. Although his coat was lighter than mine and he was just a few feet away, he'd melted into the shadows and was invisible. That reassured me. The sounds became more clear. The snapping of twigs under foot. Voices, and then little snippets of conversation floated through the underbrush. The sounds were getting louder. The patrol was heading in our direction.

I felt a sudden urge to run, but knew to keep the urge in check. If we didn't move and didn't make a sound, they'd have to step on us before they'd see us. That was how it was with all animals. An owl doesn't see a mouse until it moves. A fawn is invisible to the wolf as long as it stays completely still. It isn't the animal but the motion that's spotted. We just had to stay still.

I thought about what Tadashi and I had planned. If it looked like we were about to be discovered, it was up to me to give myself away. I'd either jump up or run off and lead them away from Tadashi. If they caught me, and I doubted they ever could, I'd just be given a big-time lecture. It might not be that easy for Tadi.

The voices became louder. I had to drive one thought out of my mind; running through the forest, soldiers crashing through the underbrush behind me, getting away, leaving them farther and farther behind, and then the crack of a bullet and a searing, burning sensation exploding in my body.

Instead I put another idea in its place. I thought about my Naani, making herself "invisible" as she glided silently through the forest, over the trip wires and between the patrols, on one of her unannounced visits to the camp to see me, my mother or Eddy.

The guards were coming closer, but it was obvious that, unless they changed course, they'd pass us on the left. The voices were now so loud I could pick out parts of the conversation. I was pretty sure I recognized one of the voices and felt reassured. They passed by at the closest point to us, and then the sounds started to fade. Soon there was silence.

I turned to Tadashi. I didn't see anything. I knew he was there, just a few feet away, squatting down low to the ground. "Tadashi!" I whispered loudly.

There was a flicker of movement and he came into focus. "That was close."

"Too close. Could you make out who it was?" I asked.

"Yeah, one of them was Washburn, wasn't it?"

"I'm pretty sure it was."

Tadashi shivered. "Do you think he would have turned us in?"

"I don't know. Maybe not, but he would have chased us away for sure. Come on, let's keep going. And remember, stay quiet."

I moved out of the underbrush and onto the trail the patrol had been following. It was the most direct line to the camp, and as long as we moved quickly, we could break off before the buildings and ahead of the next patrol circling this way. I picked up the pace and was pleased with how quietly Tadi was staying with me. We closed the distance to the camp quickly.

Up ahead was the outline of the first building. I moved to the side and we took up shelter against the wall of the structure. I pulled off my knapsack and rifle from my back and rested against the wall. Undoing the drawstrings, I removed my canteen. I offered it to Tadashi first. He took a long drink and passed it back. Tipping it to my own mouth, I was surprised by how good the water tasted and how dry my mouth had been. Fear could do that. I resealed the container and put it back into the pack. I slung the rifle over my shoulder and handed the pack to Tadashi.

Rather than going around the building, we crawled between the posts that supported it. Directly underneath the building, the ground was soft and unfrozen. My hands sunk into the muddy soil. We exited the other side of the building and came up right beneath the boardwalk.

The full view of the camp stretched out before us. The various buildings surrounded the parade ground. Each was silent and sleeping. There were no signs of light, but that wasn't surprising as each was fitted with special air-raid screens. Even if the inside was ablaze, no light would escape into the night. In the center of the parade grounds sat the darkened silhouette of Eddy's house.

"What now?" Tadashi whispered in my ear.

I kept my voice low. "We have to wait."

"For what?" he asked anxiously.

"For the guards. There are a few of them watching the inside of the camp. We have to know where they are before we do anything."

"Sounds smart. I didn't ask before, but how are we going to free Eddy?"

"Look in the pack," I said.

Tadashi pushed aside the canteen and reached in for the other objects.

"What's this?" he asked, removing a leather pouch.

"Be careful," I said, taking it from him. I unrolled it and removed a large carving knife. A tiny shard of light hit the blade and it gleamed. "It's the sharpest knife my Naani has. She uses it to skin rabbits, so I'm sure it'll go through the line."

"Do you really think Eddy will let you get close?"

"I'd think he will. I figure he'll be asleep and I'll cut it before he wakes up."

"Do eagles sleep?" Tadashi asked.

"Sure they do. Everything sleeps."

"Not everything. The fish my grandmother keeps don't even have eyelids."

"Well, eagles do," I argued. "You know that ... they must sleep." I was trying to convince myself as much as Tadashi.

"I guess you're right," Tadashi muttered. "I just don't know if it's the same way we sleep. You're going to have to get real close. You can't have him dragging a long piece of line around. It would be too dangerous for him."

"I know. I'm going to cut it right by his leg. The little bit of line left will rot off eventually. The piece of leather around his leg will do the same."

"What if he wakes up?"

"I brought along some protection." I reached over to the pack and removed a pair of heavy work gloves and pulled them on my hands. "These will help a little."

"A little is right. I think what you need is a suit of armor."

"Oh, one more thing," I said. "Here." I pulled my rifle from my shoulder and handed it to my friend. "You take this."

"Why don't we just leave it here?"

"We can't. We might need it."

"What do you mean?" he asked hesitantly.

"It's like the vet said. We won't be able to tell if he can fly until he's free. If he can't fly, we can't just let him go into the woods and we won't be able to catch him. There's no choice."

"But you won't have time to drop the gloves and grab the rifle and get him in your sight and …"

"It won't be me shooting, Tadi."

"Me!" he gasped.

"SSSSHHHHH!"

"Me," he repeated in a whisper. "Why not you? You're a much better shot."

"Not while I'm wearing gloves. I can't cut Eddy free and hold the rifle. And I think I'm the one who should cut the rope. I move quieter than you and Eddy knows me better."

"But I couldn't take a shot anyway. It would wake up everybody on the base and send the sentries right to us and we'll be caught for sure."

"We'll have a few seconds. Enough time to run straight back here and dive under the walk. I figure everybody will be looking at where Eddy used to be and we can get out the way we came."

"Yeah, but what if …"

We both heard the sounds of boots moving along

the boardwalk. I took a deep breath, like maybe I wouldn't have to breathe again until after the feet passed by. We both pulled back away from the outside edge of the walkway. The steps echoed off the wood. Then came the sound of boots against gravel. The guard was now moving along one of the paths by the parade ground. The scuffing sound was quickly replaced again by the sound of feet against wood. I felt the steps reverberating through the support beam against my side. The guard was now on the section of the walk above our heads. In the total silence of the night, the steps boomed out a steady beat, closer and closer and closer. I looked up and caught a glimpse of the sky in the slits between the boards. A shadow fell and the view was blotted out by the guard moving directly over us. Then the sky returned as he passed. Breathlessly we waited until the steps receded and he was somewhere by the outer buildings.

"Do we wait for another guard to pass?" Tadashi asked.

"No. They're spaced out so they make their rounds separately. Nobody will pass this way for a while."

"Are you sure?"

"No," I answered. "Come on. Slow and quiet. I don't want to wake up anybody ... especially Eddy."

I stood up and started across the parade ground. There was no cover and I felt exposed, visible to any eye that happened to turn in our direction. I had to fight the desire to walk quickly, even break into a run. In the darkness a slow-moving figure could blend into the background and be mistaken for shifting lights and shadows.

Coming up behind Eddy's little house, I looked around for the eagle. But Eddy was nowhere. He must be inside, sleeping, I decided. I turned back and motioned for Tadashi to go wide. I hoped he'd take up a position and get the rifle ready, just in case. I dropped to my hands and knees, clutching the knife in one hand,

and crawled around the side of the little house. I peered inside. It looked like Eddy was in there, sleeping.

This was perfect. I'd take the line where it was attached to the house and gently pull it out as far as I could. Then I'd cut it off and there'd only be a foot or two—or three at worst—still attached to his leg. I reached out and took hold of the line, right where it was anchored. My eyes followed along the rope, and with a start, I realized it didn't lead into the house. I followed the rope with my eyes. At the end of the line was Eddy, as still as a statue on his perch. He was looking straight at me. He turned his head ever so slightly to one side and a glint of light shone out of his yellow eyes. Eddy jumped down off of his perch and cautiously hopped a few feet in my direction. It took all my will to stop myself from moving backwards. I had to stay still. Eddy moved closer, opened his wings slightly and his silhouette showed his powerful beak was slightly open. He was angry and getting ready to attack or defend himself.

"Don't do that, Eddy," I croaked. "I'm here to … to … help you … to … tell you a story."

He cocked his head slightly. His beak remained open, but I could swear he'd lowered his wings, even if just slightly. "Yeah, a story," I whispered. "A story about an eagle … umm … or really it was Stoneribs dressed like an eagle … Stoneribs …" I searched my mind trying to remember things Naani mentioned about Stoneribs. "Well, old Stoneribs had got himself into some trouble. You know how he's always getting himself into trouble."

There was no mistake; Eddy had tucked his wings back in tightly against his body and his beak was closed.

"Umm … Stoneribs had been … had been captured. Yeah, he was captured. He'd been tied down with a heavy rope … like you. And now he wants to get free. But the rope is a magical rope. A rope that can only be cut by a boy … like me."

I kept my eyes locked on Eddy but reached down with my free hand and took hold of the line. I needed to pull as much of it as possible towards me.

"So the boy had to come at night, because only at night could the magic rope be cut. He had to come at night because ... because the moon ... I mean the stars, gave the knife the special powers to cut through the rope."

I felt the line become taut. Glancing down I could see the loops of rope gathered at my side. There was still five or six feet of it stretched out between me and Eddy. Too much. If he trailed that much line behind him it could tangle in a tree or get in the way of him catching food. I had to get closer. In slow motion I reached my hand forward to crawl towards him.

Eddy puffed his chest slightly, a sign he was alarmed. "It's okay, Eddy," I murmured. "So old Stoneribs, he sees this boy coming to him in the night and he sees the boy is carrying a knife ... and Stoneribs knows the boy can have that knife for two reasons: to kill Stoneribs or to free him. And Stoneribs is tied up but he's still very powerful ... like you Eddy ... and he knows he can easily hurt the boy, but he decides he won't. He decides he has to trust the boy because he hopes the boy is there to free him. But he also knows that if he's wrong, if the boy has come to kill him, it's still better than living his life tied up, unable to soar through the sky." I paused. Eddy's expression had changed. He didn't look fierce or angry, but thoughtful. "Isn't that right, Eddy? You need to live free."

I inched my one hand — the one holding the knife — forward. Closer and closer until it was no more than two feet from Eddy's foot planted in the ground. I rotated my wrist and the knife tasted the line and I could feel the fibers being severed. I worked it back and forth, back and forth. And then the knife cut into the dirt beneath the rope. The tether was cut!

"You're free, Eddy. You're free." Free to fly away or free to attack me. Slowly I withdrew my outstretched arm and started to inch away. I retreated, still on my knees, holding the knife out in front of me.

Eddy didn't move. "Come on, you're free, fly away!"

Almost as if he understood, Eddy opened his wings and leaped into the air, gliding and then landing on the peak of his little house. He wobbled back and forth and then folded up his wings and tucked his head down.

"Stupid bird," I hissed. "You're not supposed to take a nap! Shoo!" I waved my arms.

He didn't move. I picked up a rock and tossed it at the eagle. It bounced off the roof of the house noisily and hit Eddy on the leg. He gave me an angry look for a split second, then tucked his head back down against a wing.

"Jed!" Tadashi whispered urgently.

His voice brought me back to the present and I realized with a start that we couldn't stand out there in the middle of the parade grounds any longer.

"Come on," I whispered.

We hurried across the open ground until we took shelter back under the walkway. We both turned back toward Eddy.

"Why won't he fly?" Tadashi asked.

"Maybe he can't ... or maybe ... Tadi give me my rifle."

He hesitated for an instant before handing it to me.

"You better get going. No sense in both of us being here. I'll meet you by the rock ... if I can."

"I'm not going anywhere," Tadashi replied. "We started together and we end together."

I knew exactly what he meant.

I dropped to my stomach. I checked the safety; it was already off. I drew a shell into the chamber. Out in the middle of the parade grounds Eddy's dark outline, hunched atop his house, was clearly visible. Like a frozen statue he hadn't moved. I sighted the gun squarely on Eddy and then slowly, ever so slowly, lowered my aim until it was on the very peak of the roof, just below his feet. I needed the explosion to be so close it would startle Eddy and force him back to his instincts to take flight.

It was strange. I'd used this rifle so many times before, but this was the first time I'd shot to save a life. If ever this gun had magic it was needed now.

Gently I squeezed the trigger.

The bullet exploded from the gun and smashed into the wooden house. Eddy opened his wings and soared up into the sky. I scrambled out and saw him fly, a short strand of rope trailing behind him. And then he disappeared into the night sky.

"Goodbye, old man."

"Jed, come on!" Tadashi grabbed me by the shoulder.

All around us lights were coming on, and the sounds of feet against the gravel and walkways were closing in. We dove back under the walk and dropped to our knees. I followed behind Tadashi as he crawled beneath the building. I hadn't thought to sling my rifle on my shoulder and it sank beneath my hand into the mud as I scurried after him. Coming out on the other side of the building, Tadashi hesitated, waiting for me to lead. I took him by the hand and led him towards the closest stand of bush and trees.

I knew that the perimeter patrols would all be coming straight back towards the camp. All we had to do was find a place to wait while the patrols passed us by on their mad rush back to the buildings. Then we'd be free to walk away with nothing between us and safety.

It wasn't hard to avoid the patrol. We heard them crashing through the underbrush, panting and grunting and cursing in their headlong rush. They were lucky that the only Japanese within two thousand miles were friendly. I had the urge to leap out at them as they passed, just to see how high they would jump, but of course I stayed in hiding.

And then Tadashi and I walked to safety.

We came out of the forest onto the path leading between our two villages. We were almost exactly at the place we'd met, half way between the two. We hadn't spoken for the last fifteen minutes or so. I didn't know what to say, and I sensed he was lost for words as well. There was activity in the tree tops as the birds started to twitter and move around, and I could sense that sunrise was less than an hour away.

"I guess we better get home," I suggested.

He nodded his head.

"Can you write me when you get where you're going?"

"Of course, I'll write. You be sure to write back. I better be in my bed before my father gets up. He wouldn't understand how important this was."

"It was important, wasn't it?"

Tadashi nodded. "More than you know … more than you know," he said softly.

He reached out his hand and I took it in mine. I pulled him forward and wrapped my arms around him tightly. It felt good as he did the same. We both released our grips, stepped back and looked at each other. Tadi nodded his head ever so slightly, turned and walked away. I watched him move away down the path until he reached a bend, and then he was gone.

.17.

The trail was easy to follow. Broken branches, hoof prints in the moss, and blood. Lots of blood. I was surprised the buck had been able to go this far, losing this much blood.

He had a full head of antlers and I'd taken a second to admire it. Just as I'd squeezed the trigger, he'd broken to the side and I only winged it. He disappeared into a heavy stand of bush and was gone. I knew I had to follow and finish him off. It wasn't right to let an animal crawl off somewhere and slowly die.

I'd been trailing the buck for more than an hour. How much longer could he go on? It would soon be dark and the rain was starting to turn into slush. The temperature was falling as the sun started to dip into the ocean. Up ahead, I saw where the bush had been flattened. I could see it in my mind: the deer falling and then staggering to its feet once again. I bent down. There was a large pool of blood. Bright red. I dipped my finger into it; still warm. It couldn't be far away now.

Up in the sky I caught sight of a large bird. It was too far away for me to tell if it was even a bald eagle.

Nobody had said much to me about Eddy "escaping." I suspected everybody, my mother, Naani, Smitty and even the major, knew what I'd done, but as long as we didn't talk about it a lot, or I wasn't asked a direct question, we could all pretend I wasn't involved.

Rounding an outcrop of rock I came upon the buck. He wasn't any more than twenty paces ahead, lying beneath a small cedar tree. Motionless, on his side. He was already dead. I could see the large hole through the buttocks. There was a small trickle of blood still seeping out.

He was a big buck, maybe three hundred pounds. He had a beautiful set of antlers, twelve points. I could sell them down in Rupert. The American sailors loved things like that. The last set I had, and they weren't nearly this big, got me three dollars. Between the meat, the skin and the antlers, there was a lot of money lying there on the ground. Then I was struck by the thought. More than money had been there.

I shouldered my gun and took my knife from its sheath. There wouldn't be time before nightfall to get to camp and bring back men to retrieve the kill. Instead I'd have to cut down enough underbrush to cover it up, and hopefully protect it from scavengers that might otherwise make a meal of it during the night. I hacked off half a dozen low-lying branches from a neighboring cedar, and gathered them in my arms.

Turning, I was shocked to see the buck slowly lift his head off the ground and look directly at me. I was no more than five feet away. I dropped the branches. He didn't move. Large, liquid brown eyes beneath lush, long eyelashes. He didn't have the look of fear you see in wild animals on those rare occasions you get close enough to see. Nor the vacant unblinking look of the dead. He looked calm. Maybe even thoughtful, like something important was going on inside his head. He knew I was here to end his life. But the buck also sensed this was the only rescue from the pain. He blinked and I blinked back. His tongue hung out of the side of his mouth, which was coated with a thick lathering of white foam. He shook his head, ever so slightly, and the foam sprayed into the air.

I unshouldered my rifle and took aim. The buck looked at me through unwavering eyes. I wanted to look away. I closed my eyes and lowered the gun. I wished I'd never found him or hit him, or somehow I could help him. I knew there was only one way to help.

I raised the gun and fired. The bullet smashed into the buck a split second before the explosion of sound reached my ears. The head instantly flopped to the ground and there was quiet. I turned away, put down my rifle and once again began to gather the branches to cover up the carcass.

After placing the branches so the buck was completely covered, I took rocks and positioned them to pin the branches in place. Before starting back I had one final task. I took one of the red markers out of my bag and tied it securely to one of the branches above the buck.

Glancing up I realized I'd been so intent upon tracking the deer I hadn't been paying attention to where I was. Looking around, I knew. Just off to the east I saw the high rocks marking the back door of Sikima. I hadn't been there for three weeks. I'd tried not to even think about it. Now it was right between me and home.

For a split second I thought about taking a longer route home to avoid the village completely. I knew this didn't make any sense, especially with night closing in. I decided to take the most direct route over the rocky outcrop.

Starting to climb I couldn't help but think about Tadashi. When we were little, we spent a lot of time in these rocks, playing and pretending. The last couple of years we'd go up there to sit and talk and watch. We could see the whole village, the harbor and the approaches from the open ocean. Even on the hottest summer day, there was always a cool breeze blowing in off the water.

By the time I reached the top, I'd worked up a sweat. I sat down on my favorite outcrop and let my feet hang over the edge, fifty feet above the bottom. I removed my knapsack and pulled out my canteen. I took a long, cool drink. It felt good in my mouth and then down my parched throat.

Stretched out before me was Sikima. All of the houses were painted and pretty and perfectly still. It felt like I was looking at a painting. There was no motion, or sound or life. It didn't seem real. I could see Tadashi's home. The small wooden building, painted light blue, curtains pulled shut, the garden plot neatly furrowed, waiting for next year's planting, the front door closed. So many times I'd walked up that pathway and been welcomed into their home. Now it was empty.

All the houses were empty. That thought echoed around my head the way footsteps echo through an empty room. All of those people; those I cared for, those I knew, heck, even people like Toshio; they were all gone. Nothing left but ghosts living in perfectly preserved little houses. I felt numb. The kind of feeling you get when your foot falls asleep, but this was inside my whole head.

Sitting there in silence, I heard only sounds of the gentle rain and the lapping of the waves against the shore. Then, ever so faintly, another sound intruded; a motor. I wasn't alone with the ghosts. But where was the sound coming from? Who was it?

Almost on cue a small boat rounded the outstretched finger of land protecting the harbor from the open water. It was a fishing boat. The deck was empty except for a small covered bridge for the captain to take refuge from the weather. In the fading light I could make out two or three people moving around. The noise of the engine, which got louder as the boat got closer, was punctuated by the sound of loud conversation.

It moved across the empty harbor. Just out from the

him by the arm and started to pull him back. The other two dropped their bags.

"Stay together, and get back to your boat," I ordered.

Wordlessly, without looking back, they moved down the center of the street. I stayed a dozen paces behind them, my gun at the ready. When they reached the dock, two jumped into the boat and the other two started to untie the ropes.

"Wait," I ordered one of the men. He stopped and looked up from the rope.

"You're native," I said.

"Yeah."

"I've never met a native who did things like this."

He just shrugged his shoulders and untied the knot. Then he jumped on the boat without looking at me again.

I locked eyes with the bearded man already on the boat.

"Big hero, aren't you, kid. Big deal. So you stop us for now. We'll be back, or somebody else will. What are you going to do, stand guard for the rest of the war?"

"Maybe. But before you go, I want the other bags back. The ones you put on the boat already."

"Don't push your luck," he snarled.

My gun was aimed off to the side of his head. I fired. The bullet whizzed by and shattered the bridge's wind screen. He jumped backwards and I saw a splattering of blood. He'd been hit by flying glass.

"Now," I demanded as I pumped another shell into the chamber.

Without uttering another word he tossed the bags onto the dock.

"Get going," I ordered.

The engine roared to life and they pushed away from the dock. The gap of water between us opened up, and the bearded man motioned for one of the others to take the wheel. He walked to the back of the boat.

"I won't forget you, kid!" he screamed. "You better watch out … maybe the next time I'll be the one with the gun!"

I turned and walked away. He continued to yell, but his voice became quieter as the boat steamed away. Soon all that remained was silence. All at once my legs become rubbery. I slumped to the ground and rested my back against the storage shed. My hands were shaking and a cold sweat poured out of my body. Holding the gun tightly against my chest, I found myself rocking. What now? He was right, I couldn't stay here forever.

"Maybe not forever," I said to myself out loud, "but at least for tonight."

I got to my feet and opened the door to the storage shed. I took the two bags and placed them on the dirt floor of the shed. Next I found a canvas tarp and tucked it under my arm. I closed the door behind me and moved back to the rock face. I climbed to my familiar perch. I pulled the collar of my jacket up around my neck. I felt a terrible chill, but I knew this was coming from within, not from the weather.

At least tonight the village would be safe.

.18.

I awoke with a start. For an instant I had no idea where I was. Then it all came back. I shifted my weight, and shook the tarp I'd used as a blanket. I was still clutching my rifle. I had held it tightly in my hand all through the night. As I stood up and stretched, thick drops of dew slid down the tarp and dropped off the bottom. My back felt all kinky and I worked my legs slowly up and down.

There was a thick mist coating the village and the harbor was not visible at all. I slowly looked around, trying to see if anybody was there. Everything was still and silent. In the daylight, even the faint, fog-shrouded daylight, it seemed better. All through the night I'd been jarred awake at every sound and shudder of the dark. Now things seemed, if not safe, at least safer.

I uncurled my fingers from the rifle and set it down at my feet. I took the tarp, gave it a good shake, folded it up and put it under the overhang. I placed a rock on top to weigh it down and keep it there. There was no telling when I might need it again. Besides, I didn't want to leave the rocks again to go down into the village. There was no telling who was hiding where.

I started for the base. I was pretty sure nobody had missed me last night. My mother would have assumed I'd gone back to Naani's for the night, while Naani would have figured I was spending another night at the camp.

Very deliberately I decided I didn't want to go through the village. I climbed down the side of the rock face closest to the camp. Although it would take a little longer, I'd backtrack the route I'd followed chasing the deer. I knew it was stupid but I kept on picturing those guys putting into shore just up the coast and hiding, waiting for me to pass. In the forest I'd be safe even from my imagination.

I passed right by the buck. I could see the cover was still in place. Nothing had disturbed it during the night. The trail was easy to follow and I made time. It felt good to put distance between me and the village.

Despite the cold morning air, I felt myself working up a sweat. I stopped and undid my jacket. Through a break in the forest cover, in the distance, I saw a thick chimney of smoke rising straight up into the air. It was a beacon, from the fire pit, directing me to the camp. I doubled my pace. It was important to do something quickly.

Soon I was on the very outskirts of the camp. I gingerly climbed over the low trip wire that completely encircled the base. Moving quickly and noisily, I caught the attention of one of the guard patrols. Both men waved a greeting and I waved back.

I came out on the opposite site of the camp from the major's office. I crossed through the middle of the parade ground. Eddy's perch sat empty and a smile creased my face. I walked directly to the major's office. Without hesitating, I knocked.

"Come!"

I opened the door. The major was seated, and three of his officers were hunched over his desk, studying whatever was on top.

"Yes, Jed?" Major Brown asked.

"I need to talk to you, sir."

"I am sorry, Jed, but I'm in conference for at least

the first half of the day. Can you come back sometime after lunch?"

"It's important."

"What we're doing is important too!" snapped Captain Stevenson, glaring at me.

There was a pregnant silence. "Important?" Major Brown asked.

"Yes, sir."

He nodded. "Let's take a short break. Gentlemen, why don't you go and have a coffee in the mess hall. I'll send for you when Jed and I have concluded our talk."

"Sure thing," replied one.

"No problem, a break would be nice," added another.

Stevenson remained silent but continued to glare at me as he followed the other two out the door.

"Please, have a seat, Jed."

"Thanks," I mumbled. "I'm sorry, I didn't mean to interrupt ..." I let the sentence trail off.

"That's not a problem. But something else is?"

"I was over by the village last night. I shot a deer. And ... and, there were men there ... they were breaking into the houses ... taking things."

"Did you get a good look at them?"

"Yeah, really good."

"Did they see you?"

"Yes, sir. They were almost as close to me as you are. I forced them to leave the village," I said, my voice trailing off.

There was a look of concern on Major Brown's face. "Jed, how did you force them to leave?"

"I aimed my weapon, sir. I told them to go ... or else."

"Were you prepared to make good on that threat?"

"I don't know ... but I couldn't just let them do what they were doing. I couldn't just let them break into houses and steal other people's things ... Tadashi's family's things ... I just couldn't let them."

"Never point a gun at a man unless you are prepared to discharge it. Would you have fired?"

"I don't know. Maybe."

He rose from his seat, circled around and sat on the very edge of his desk, right in front of me. "Give me your gun."

I removed it from my shoulder and handed it to him.

"This was your grandfather's, right?"

"Yes, sir."

He stood and held the gun. He raised it and looked down the sights. "It is a beautiful old gun. Your grandfather must have trusted you very much to have left it to you." He paused and sat back down on his desk, the rifle cradled in his lap. "What you did last night, confronting those men, was stupid and dangerous … and brave."

He handed me back my rifle. "I thank you for sharing this with me. I trust your judgment, Jed. I'm sure you did what you felt you had to do."

I nodded my head slowly. "It's just I wouldn't want to come back to my house and have my stuff broken or missing. Things have been rough enough for them. I wanted everything to be the same as when they left, so Tadashi can walk into his house and it'll be just like before."

The major abruptly got up from his seat and walked across the room, stopping by the window. I watched him in silence for half a minute or more, my nervousness growing by the second. Just as I felt I couldn't wait any longer, he came back and sat on the edge of his desk again.

"Jed, you need to know that things will never be the same."

"I know, but I still hope."

"I understand why you would hope, but there are things you aren't aware of which make that hope an impossibility."

"What do you mean?"

"I shouldn't be telling you any of this … no one is to be told," he said solemnly. "But I'm going to tell you in strictest confidence. You cannot repeat any of this to anyone. Do you understand?"

I nodded.

"Orders have come down. The contents of those houses, and the houses themselves, will be declared the property of the Canadian government and put under the control of the Custodian of Alien Property. Everything will be confiscated and the previous owners will be compensated."

"I don't understand … confiscated … compensated?"

"The government has decided to take away the houses, fishing boats and all possessions of the former inhabitants," Major Brown explained. "They will be given money in exchange."

"There's no way the Fukushimas would ever sell their home!"

"They have no choice. The decision has been made. They say it's for the protection of our country. Do you understand?"

"No," I said defiantly. "I don't understand any of it. Why do they have to take away his house … how is his family a threat to this country?"

"I don't understand all of it myself, Jed. I wish I had answers, but I don't. I don't." He paused. "Could you go to the mess and ask my officers to join me?" he requested.

I stood up and started for the door before spinning around.

"But, Major, they said they'd be back or others would be back. We have to stop them," I pleaded.

"I'm sorry, Jed, but there isn't anything I can do. Guarding the villages is the job of the RCMP. I know they don't have the manpower to do it very effectively, but I can't do anything about it. And, as I explained,

Tadashi and his family and all the others will soon no longer even own the houses or the contents of those houses."

"But …"

Major Brown rose from the corner of his desk. He walked over and placed his hands on my shoulders. "Jed, this isn't right, no more than it was right to chase those people out of their homes in the first place, but there's nothing we can do. Nothing. I'll make a full report to the Commander of the RCMP detachment, and we have to leave it with him. I am sorry, believe me."

As I left his office, I felt tears welling up in my eyes. I wanted to be alone. I was too big to be seen bawling. Halfway across the parade grounds it hit me.

Maybe I couldn't protect the whole village. But I could do something.

.19.

"I should have my head examined," Smitty said as he put the eight-wheeled, all-terrain buggy into motion. Attached to the back was a trailer. We started out through the main gate.

"Smitty, we have to go in the other direction."

"I know where the village is, Jed, but I also know it's best to head in another direction first. You can't even believe how serious this is … and how much trouble we can get into."

"How serious is it?" I asked.

"Serious enough to get you kicked off the base and me thrown in the brig with my stripe taken away."

"I'm sorry for getting you involved. I just couldn't think of any other way."

Smitty grimaced. "Neither could I and, believe me, I tried."

Travel with the buggy was slow. Smitty had to find paths around the rocks and between the trees and brush that were wide enough to accommodate the vehicle. While it wasn't very wide — the two of us sat scrunched up side by side — it still took more room than what was often there. As well, despite the eight wheels gripping for traction, the inclines and bogs were often too much for it to handle. We had to crisscross through the forest, Smitty looking for a route, while I tried to keep us aimed in about the right direction. We agreed we'd get the buck I'd shot loaded up before we went any further. Smitty said the buck would be our "beard" if anyone stumbled on us when we first reached the village. I didn't know what he meant by a "beard," but he explained it was a disguise to cover up other things.

Most of the time we rode in silence. This wasn't like Smitty and I knew he was nervous. I was nervous as well.

"Up ahead, you see the rocks just by the village?" I asked, pointing at about two o'clock. "The buck is just to this side of the cliff, so head straight at it."

Soon we were on the trail I'd used twice; once following the deer and the second time coming back to camp. Rounding the last corner, the cover, anchored down and marked with the red flag, was clearly visible. Smitty pulled up right in front and then began jockeying the buggy back and forth to position the trailer as close as possible to the buck. We both climbed out and started removing the cover.

"Looks all right," I commented. "I don't think anything got into it." If not for the gaping bullet hole I could have believed it was just sleeping.

"Big one," Smitty said.

"Do you think we'll be able to get it up onto the trailer?" I asked, realizing there usually were at least two other people with me to help with that task.

"Don't worry. Where muscle fails, we need to use brains."

Smitty started to pull rope and pulleys out of the trailer. He flung one end of the rope over a branch above the carcass. He gathered in the end and fed it into a pulley.

"Is there anything I can do to help?" I asked.

"Nope. What you could do is go under the front seat of the buggy. I had your mother pack us a few sandwiches and a thermos of coffee. A coffee would go good right now. It's getting cool."

I followed his directions. I opened the thermos and a cloud of warm steam escaped into the air. I poured a cup and resealed it to keep the rest hot. Smitty hooked the rope around the buck's neck and started to use the pulley to raise it off the ground. I stood and watched, holding his coffee. Without too much effort Smitty slowly lifted the buck off the ground. The overhead branch sagged and creaked but held as the carcass was lifted into the air. He continued to haul the rope through the pulley system until the deer was level with the trailer. He then tied the rope in place using a knot which would release with one tug. He walked toward me and took the coffee, taking a sip.

"Your turn now. Move the buggy so the trailer is right underneath while I finish my coffee."

I climbed aboard and settled into the driver's seat. I turned the key in the ignition and the engine sparked to life. I had only driven the buggy once before. The gears on it were different than a truck or car, and I fumbled around trying to find reverse. I let out the clutch and rocketed forward instead and it stalled out. I didn't even want to look at Smitty. I started again and found reverse. What made things even more confusing was the action of the trailer. It seemed to turn the opposite way to what I thought it would. Slowly, moving back and forth, I got it to bump into, and then under the buck. I looked back at Smitty and he gave me a thumbs up.

He put the cup down on the dashboard of the vehicle and walked around to where he'd tied off the rope. He undid the knot and lowered the deer into the flatbed of the trailer. He pulled one end of the rope out from under the deer, disconnected the pulley and threw all the equipment into the back alongside the buck.

"That was easy," I observed.

"Brains over brute force. Usually you bring a couple

of the guys who are big on muscle power but short on mental power."

"No one could argue you don't have brain power."

Smitty laughed. "Anybody who knew I was even thinking about going along with you on this little outing would figure I was brain dead."

"It's good nobody knows," I said.

"Too late for that."

I gave him a questioning gaze.

"I told your mother."

My mouth dropped open. "You told my mother!"

"Yeah. I wasn't going to have any part of this without her knowing. And if you don't like it, too bad, so don't give me that look!"

I tried to regain my composure. "What did she say? Did she get mad?"

"You know your mother. She didn't say a lot. She said to be careful and if anything happened to you she'd make sure I never ate at the camp again."

"But she didn't say we shouldn't do it?"

"No," he answered, "but she didn't say we should do it either. She just said we should be careful."

"Good. Come on, let's get going. It's dark enough to provide some cover. Did you bring along flashlights?"

"Flashlights?" Smitty replied. "I thought you'd bring them."

I walked away over to the buggy and rummaged around under the passenger side seat. I pulled out a box, and flipped open the lid to reveal, amongst other things, two large flashlights.

"You can't fool me all the time. No way you'd ever leave the camp unprepared."

Smitty smiled and then climbed in behind the wheel. "Jed, my boy, you're getting older and wiser."

He turned the key and started us forward. "Which way around this pile of rocks?"

"Swing to the right. It's longer but I think it'll be easier."

I felt my stomach tighten as we rocked and bumped over the rough ground. I was very glad Smitty was with me. Not just for the company or to help but because I knew I couldn't back out. I said it, and now I had to do it.

We entered the village along the familiar path between it and my Naani's village.

Almost as if on cue, clouds rolled over top and sealed out the moon and the stars. The only illumination was from the headlights of the buggy. The houses, fences and sheds all cast shadows when the light touched each in turn as we rolled down the center of the street. The engine drowned out any hint of other sounds, including the roar of the ocean. I felt like we were being watched from every window. I yelled out directions to Smitty and we came to a stop in front of Tadashi's home. He turned off the engine and I was struck by the silence of the village. I climbed out immediately. Smitty stayed seated behind the wheel and moved his head to look all around.

"Even in the dark it looks like a pretty little place," Smitty noted. "So, what's the plan, boss?"

"Could you go down to the dock? If there's anybody here, they probably would have come by boat."

"So, no boats, no people. What are you going to do?"

"I'm going to go into the house," I replied solemnly.

Smitty leaned over and pulled out the two flashlights. He handed one to me and, taking the second, climbed out of the vehicle. Smitty snapped on his flashlight and a powerful beam swept out before him, lighting a path. He followed the light in the direction of the waves washing into the shore.

I turned on my light. Its beam flooded through the gate, up the path and splashed onto the front door of Tadashi's house. Walking up the path, I glanced to the side at the faint images of the delicate shrubs filling the garden. Deliberately I didn't train my light anywhere other than the path. The shapes of the shrubs seemed spooky. I thought of spirits.

The windows were dark and the curtains drawn. I stopped and knocked on the door. I knew nobody was home, but it just seemed like the right thing to do. I turned the knob and swung the door open. Stepping across the threshold, I swept the beam around the room. I was relieved to see everything was still in place. Nothing had been disturbed. I'd expected to find things missing or destroyed.

"Hello … is anybody here?" I called out. I didn't expect to get a reply but wanted to have the company of my voice. The walls and empty air absorbed my words. I moved through the house, room by room. Everything was so normal I almost expected to see Tadi and his family sleeping peacefully in their beds. Somehow that made it even harder. I felt like I was the looter, like I was the one violating their home. Maybe I could just leave and nobody would break in and take their belongings. In my head I knew this was a lie. I knew that whatever I didn't take would be lost, either to the looters or to the government.

I had to make some decisions. I couldn't take everything so I had to take the most important things. The dining room table stood off to my side. I walked over and sat down, folding my legs underneath. I turned the flashlight off and sat in the darkness. I had to think through my next steps.

I heard sounds behind me and turned to see a ray of light coming up the path.

"Hello!" Smitty called out.

"I'm over here."

"Where?" he asked, sweeping the beam of light around the room until it found me. "Why don't you have your flashlight on? Is it broken?"

I switched the light back on. "No, I just wanted darkness for a minute to think. Are there any boats?"

"Nobody there," he began. "How come you haven't started loading?"

"I can't decide what to take."

"It would be hard," Smitty agreed. "You're trying to decide for people who aren't even here, what they'd want you to take. I think what you have to do is look for things that can't be replaced, that are important to them. Not necessarily worth much money but valuable in other ways."

I rose from the table, unfolding my legs. I remembered the first time I'd sat squat-legged at this table. The dozens and dozens of other times I'd shared much more than a meal with this family filled my mind.

"I know where to start." I went to the head of the table. "Pick up the other end."

"The table?"

"Yes, the table."

We maneuvered it out through the door and placed it carefully on its side on the trailer beside the buck.

Over the next hour we went back and removed pictures from the walls, sleeping mats, a delicate oriental screen, a mantle clock, clothing they hadn't been able to take, and, most important, dishes and serving bowls.

Smitty went outside to make sure everything was tied down, while I made a last minute search of the house. The beam of light moved around the room, hunting out corners and hidden spots. Moving one last time through Tadashi's room, I saw something partially hidden in the corner of the closet. It was his baseball glove. I thought of the hours we played ball together. I picked it up and tucked it under my arm.

The noise of the buggy starting up outside jarred me into motion. I made my way to the front door and then turned off the flashlight. Looking back, I could make out very little in the sudden and total darkness. I didn't want to see what remained but to remember what once was. In the darkness I could imagine Tadi and his family safely in their beds, their belongings filling their house, and I could come back again tomorrow. But I knew it would never be the same. I knew I'd never walk in this house again. My mother was right. Some things were just too big. Once they'd been done, they could never be undone.

"Goodbye," I said softly. I closed the door for the final time.

•••

The path between Sikima and my house was fairly straight and flat. Smitty opened up the buggy, getting it all the way up to third gear. In less than ten minutes we were passing the first house on the outskirts of my village. It was a broken down little house, as crooked as the old man, my grandmother's cousin, who lived there. The lights showing in the windows were welcome signs of life.

Smitty changed gears, slowing us down, and then brought us to a stop in front of my Naani's place. The curtains in the front window were drawn, but there was still light leaking out along the edges.

"Does your grandmother realize how much stuff we're bringing?" Smitty asked.

"No, not really. Actually she doesn't know we're bringing anything."

"What?"

"Don't worry, there won't be any problem. There's never a problem with my Naani. Come on, you'll see." I bounded out of the buggy.

I pushed open the door. "Naani, I'm home!" Smitty followed in behind me.

Naani came out of the kitchen.

"Hello, grandson. I see you brought your friend. Hello, Smitty. Come, both of you, into the kitchen and I'll put on a pot of tea."

"Thanks, Naani, but before we do that we have a few things to bring in from the buggy."

"Things, what kind of things?" she asked. I had already explained about the looters to her before I headed to school this morning.

"From Tadashi's house," I said quietly.

"Much?"

"Afraid so," Smitty replied.

She walked out of the living area into the kitchen. I followed after her and Smitty followed me. I felt a deadening in my chest. What if she wouldn't let me store the things here? What would I do with them? I couldn't, or I guess, wouldn't put them back now. She walked over to the stove, picked up the kettle, and filled it. She placed it on one of the burners of the stove and flicked a match to light the burner.

"What kind of tea ya like, Smitty?" she asked.

"Any kind is fine."

"Jed, show him the kinds we got and then make what he wants. I'll be back. I want to see the stuff you brought."

As I walked over to the cupboard, my mind raced outside to be with Naani. I wanted to follow, but I knew she was going out there to think. Smitty chose the tea he wanted. He didn't care what he drank, as long as it didn't smell like "perfume." We sat in silence until the whistling of the kettle announced the water was ready. I poured a little bit of the boiling water into the teapot, rolled it around to get the teapot all warm, and then dumped the water down the drain. I put the leaves of the tea inside the tea ball, put it in the pot and poured in the water. Just as I put the empty kettle down, I heard the front door open. Smitty eyed me with a "what now?" expression. I wished I had the answer to his question.

"Jed," Naani called, "when you and Smitty finish you come help."

"Help?" Smitty and I said in unison.

We rushed to our feet. We moved to the door and were greeted at the threshold by the sight of my Naani holding the mantle clock.

"House not too big. Better make sure we put things in a safe place."

Then my cousin Jonnie came in carrying a sleeping mat.

"Hi, Jed, nice buck."

"Thanks, Jonnie," I answered. "It was a hard kill."

No sooner had I finished replying when the door opened again and Peter pushed in with another one of the mats.

"Hi, Jed. You did the right thing." For Peter that was practically a speech.

They both nodded to Smitty.

"Come on, put that stuff down in Jed's room and get moving," Naani chided. "If I know you fellas, you's all stand there gabbing and let the old woman do all the work."

•••

In a matter of only a few minutes we unloaded everything, while Naani remained inside directing. As we worked we were joined by another half-dozen of my relatives, some of whom watched, but most carried at least one thing inside. I introduced Smitty to each of them as they came forward. With the last item inside, I excused Smitty and myself, explaining we had to get back with the buck right away, so we wouldn't get into trouble. We climbed into the buggy and started along the path to the camp.

"Aren't you afraid somebody's going to tell what you did?" Smitty asked.

"Nope. I can't even imagine that."

"I guess it helps when most of them are relatives. Cripes, it seems like you're related to almost everybody in the whole village," Smitty commented.

"Not almost everybody ... everybody."

"Everybody?"

"Everybody. My Naani can explain how we're all related. She can tell stories about everybody's ancestors for three generations back, and then stories from the beginning of her people."

"Her people? Don't you mean your people?"

"Yeah ... I guess that is what I mean."

Smitty slowly shook his head and a smile came to his face. "Must be nice, Jed, must really be nice."

"What do you mean?" I questioned.

"You know, to have a place like this ... where you belong."

.20.

"Naani, I'm home!" I yelled as I came in from school.

"Hello, Jed," she answered as she came out of the kitchen. Sometimes I swear she lives in there. If I didn't come home, she'd curl up on the table and go to sleep right there beside the stove.

"Anything good to eat?"

"Always. Look in the ice box. School's supposed to make you smarter. With you I only see it making you hungry."

"Are you kidding, old woman, learning is what makes a guy hungry. I learned so much today I could eat a bear."

"The eating part I see. Feel like learning some more today?"

"Naw, I don't think you have enough food in the house."

"Okay," she replied, walking across the room away from me. "If you don't want to learn what's in this letter, that's okay."

"Letter! A letter from Dad?"

She held it aloft in her hand. "A letter, yes. From your Dad, no."

"From who? Who sent me a letter?" I raced across the room with my hand outstretched and she stuffed the envelope into the pocket of her apron.

"We won't find out 'til tomorrow, what with you being

all learned out and us not having a bear for you to eat."

"Naani! Come on!"

She chuckled, pulled the letter back out and handed it to me. I recognized the handwriting instantly. It was from Tadashi. I tore open the envelope, ripping the corner of the letter. I was about to start reading it, when I glanced up and saw her still hovering around.

"How about if I read it out loud?"

"If you want."

I knew she wanted me to. "Okay, here I go."

Dear Jed,

Sorry I didn't have a chance to write earlier but it's not so easy to send a letter. All mail, in and out, is read by the soldiers who guard us. I've seen what they do to letters. They use big markers and just black out anything they don't think anybody should know. They don't think anybody should know anything. I got away for an hour and mailed this from a mailbox away from the park so they couldn't get their hands on it.

That's right, I'm living in a park; Hastings Park, in Vancouver. I always thought Vancouver would be pretty exciting. Mostly what we see are the fences surrounding the park. You can get out if you're sneaky, but we're supposed to stay inside. Besides, my parents don't think it's safe to be Japanese and out in the city. The newspapers are full of stories of the war and they're afraid we might be attacked on the streets.

After the trip down here I don't fear getting attacked. Nothing could be worse than what we went through. It took us fifteen days. All the fishing boats were tied together behind two navy frigates. There were sixty boats. The seas were heavy and there was a lot of fog.

Our boat became covered in ice from the spray. We had to chip it off. The only place to get away from the cold and spray was in the cabin. You know how small that is, but somehow we managed to find places to sleep. There were times I wasn't sure we'd make it.

I heard afterwards they probably brought our boat up to the Annieville Dyke on the Fraser River. Somebody told me they have twelve hundred Japanese fishing boats all tied up there. I think it causes my father great distress to know how his boat is being cared for—or really uncared for. He said if he knew what was going to happen to it he would have sunk it himself.

The boat ride prepared us for living in a small space. My family has been given a stall to live in. I don't mean a small place. I mean a stall. We're living in the place where they used to show livestock. All of us families have been given a separate stall, and we've hung blankets and things to act as curtains. So I guess if somebody ever asks me if I was raised in a barn, I can answer yes.

I can kid about it, but it really steams me to be treated like cattle. A lot of us, mostly Canadian born, are really angry. There's a lot of talk about a protest, or petition or civil disobedience, or something. Nothing has come of it. My father tells me not to get involved. None of the Issei seem to want to get involved.

My father is typical of how they're acting. He walks around with his eyes on the ground. Best I can make out he feels shamed by his treatment. Can you imagine that? These people make us leave our homes, and he figures he's the one who should be ashamed! The people who should feel ashamed are those politicians

*who ordered our internment and the RCMP officers
who did it. So much for democracy and the British
sense of fair play. Can you tell me where the fairness is?*

*I don't know for sure, but I figure there must be close
to five thousand people living here. They cook big
meals for all of us or we can fix some things in our
stall. There's only a couple of showers and a few more
washrooms for the whole place.*

*There isn't much to do. When the weather changes
there'll be more things. There's a baseball diamond,
some woods and a soccer field. Fortunately, or maybe
not so fortunately, we probably won't be here when
that happens.*

*There's lots of rumors going around. I heard they're
going to ship us across Canada, away from the coast.
Another rumor is that we're bound for Japan. Some
other people said the war will be over before spring
comes and they'll let us go home. Another rumor is
that we don't even have homes to go to, our houses
were being taken apart by looters. Other talk is that
we don't even own the homes any more, that the
government is taking them away. Who knows? It
would make me feel better if you could just go by my
place, and make sure everything is okay. You can
write me back at Hastings Park, Exhibition Building,
Vancouver. Please tell me how you're doing and how
things are going around Rupert.*

> *Your friend always,
> Tadashi*

*p.s. You'll get another letter from me in a day. That's
so the censors will see me writing to you and won't get
suspicious when you write back.*

p.p.s. Be careful what you write. They read all the letters coming in as well as going out.

p.p.p.s. They got me acting like I really am a spy.

"That's it."

"A stall … that don't seem right … treating them like cattle," she said as she shook her head soulfully.

I felt a sense of rage inside of me.

"Who you angry at?" she asked.

"I'm not …" I started to lie, "… I mean I don't know." Maybe she couldn't read a letter but she could read a person's spirit like it was an open book.

"Don't get sad and mad, all confused. You got to tell him about what's happening. You got to answer his questions."

"I know. I just don't know how to do it."

"Just tell him," she replied.

"I can't. I mean, even if I can put it into words okay, those censor guys wouldn't let him read it. Besides, if they read about me taking all his family's stuff, then I could get in big trouble. Smitty and you too. How can I let him know?"

"Ha … don't worry. You got yourself a smart Naani. I figure it out while you write him."

"I wish I could be that sure."

"Jed, have I ever let you down?"

"Well …" actually she never had. "No."

"Sit, write, I get you a little food to help your brain work." She retreated to her kitchen.

"Start your letter by saying we figured out to get this letter to him so nobody gonna know," she yelled from the kitchen.

I pulled a note pad and a pen out of my pack. I walked over to the couch and leaped into the air. The springs groaned loudly as I landed.

"Take it easy on the furniture!" she hollered.
I started to write.

Dear Tadashi,

We figured out a way to write to you so the censors wouldn't see it. I was really glad to get your letter. I'm sorry about how things worked out and about where you're living. Things here aren't the same without you. School is more boring, although with all the Japanese gone, the teachers now see me as being a good student. Hard to imagine, me a good student. I spend more time at home now that they hired a second cook.

My mom and Naani are okay. I still worry about my father. He writes letters and tells us there's nothing to worry about, but I know what he's doing is about as dangerous as you can get. I'm also very proud of him. I heard, not from him, of course, that he's an ace, which means he's shot down at least five enemy planes.

I keep an eye out for Eddy. I haven't seen him, but one of the guards is sure he saw him.

I'm sorry to be the one to have to tell you, but some of those rumors are true. I was out at your village two weeks ago. I was tracking a big buck. I got into the village and found some guys breaking into the houses. I chased them off, but they said they'd be back. I heard from the soldiers that looting has been taking place all over. Major Brown said the RCMP doesn't have the people to stop them. Anyway, I figured that though I couldn't stop everything, I could stop them from taking your stuff. I went and collected a lot of your belongings, things I thought your family would

want. They're safe and I'll get them to your family as
soon as you know where you're going to.

I'm really sorry for all that's happened. Please let your
family know that most of the people, even people like
Major Brown, figure what they did to you was wrong.
I just hope it won't be wrong for too long.

> *Your best friend,*
> *Jed*

p.s. Write again soon.

I put my legs down on the floor and sat up on the couch. Naani was standing at the doorway to my bedroom, wearing Tadi's baseball glove on the wrong hand and kind of pounding her fist in the pocket the way she'd probably seen me doing with my glove.

"Here," she called out, tossing the glove in my general direction.

It soared off, nowhere within my reach and bashed into a picture on the table, knocking it to the floor.

"Try to be more careful," she scolded me in a mocking tone.

I picked up the glove and put the picture back on the table.

"Nice baseball hand thing."

"Glove, it's called a glove, Naani."

"Yeah, glove. Nice glove ... but better envelope."

"Envelope? What do you mean?"

"Look. What was the first thing you did when you got the glove?"

It was sitting snugly on my hand.

"And what do ya think Tadashi will do, first thing, when he gets that glove in the mail?" she asked.

A smile came to my face. "Put it on, of course," I laughed. "And when he does, he'll find this letter all crunched up in the tip of one of the fingers."

"Right."

"But, what if they won't let him have the glove?"

"A gun they don't let him have. A radio, or camera they keep. Maybe even a knife, no way. A glove, yes. Just write a little letter to him that says nothin except you thought he might like 'your old glove' and put it in a parcel with the glove. Nobody will figure it out," she said.

"Naani, I think you're right."

"'Course I'm right. Haven't I told ya, you don't get this old without getting smart."

I got up off the couch and threw my arms around her shoulders. I couldn't even imagine a time when she hadn't been smart.

.21.

I exhaled deeply and watched my breath float up and into the sky. It was a crisp morning, but there was a hint of spring in the air. I'd seen a few animals — a momma skunk leading a few kittens and a raccoon — but nothing there was any point in taking a shot at. Funny, despite the lack of success, it still felt good just to be out in the forest, amongst the trees and on my own. Before, a good hunt was marked only by the game I'd brought down or put in my bag. Somehow things had changed. I had to smile; that's the way my grandfather always talked and I never understood what he meant. Now I knew that to be amongst the trees was reward enough.

In the distance, well up above the trees, a large bird floated on the air currents. I pulled my pack off my shoulders and removed a pair of army field glasses that Major Brown had given me. He said with those I could still try to "keep an eye out" for Eddy. They were very powerful and at first I found them difficult to get in focus and sighted on the target, but I was getting better with them all the time. I scanned the sky until the bird came into view. It was a golden eagle. I followed its circular course, supported by the thermals, until suddenly it dropped down in a dive and was lost in the trees below my sight line. I put the glasses down but left them dangling on my neck.

Since Eddy had gone, I'd become much more aware

of the sky. There always seemed to be a raven, a hawk or an eagle on the horizon. Usually they were too far away to see very well, even with the field glasses, but a couple of times I was close enough to be able to tell it wasn't Eddy. So far I hadn't seen a bald eagle trailing a small piece of rope from one of its feet. Naani told me she was sure someone would see him. And once, although I was so far away it could have been the light playing tricks with my eyes, I thought I saw something hanging below an eagle.

As well, as the weeks passed it became more likely that even if it was Eddy, he would have freed himself of the line. I can just picture that old buzzard pecking and pecking away at the rope. He was one stubborn old ... I had to chuckle ... he did share more with my grandfather than just a liking for rabbit. Not that I believe all those native stories, but if my grandfather could come back to life it would be as an eagle.

Naani had told me to stop spending so much time staring up at the sky; there weren't any rabbits or deer up there. She had a point. I hadn't been bagging nearly the game I did before. I'd told her how I wanted to try and see Eddy and she tried to explain how I still had things backwards; it wasn't me who was supposed to watch out for the eagle, but the eagle who was supposed to be watching out for me.

She was even more insistent than before that Eddy was my grandfather. She was so certain, she said she didn't need to worry about me when I went into the forest alone, because no spirits could harm me.

I couldn't help but miss my father and grandfather and, of course, Tadashi. I think I missed him the most. For the last eight months he'd written me letters and I wrote back, but it couldn't be the same as before. His family had settled in Alberta, where they were working on a farm growing sugar beets. He didn't tell me much about what was happening to them, but he wrote enough for me to know life was hard.

At first we both wrote in our letters about the time when he could return. Then we just hinted at it. Now we both knew he wouldn't be coming back for a long time. Maybe never. I'd heard the looting had continued and more than just things had been taken. The houses themselves were being damaged and destroyed. I hadn't returned to Sikima since the night I removed Tadashi's family belongings. I couldn't bring myself to go back.

My gaze was caught again by an outline of a bird in the sky. As I watched, it circled closer and closer until it was directly overhead. It was close enough now for me to be certain it was a bald eagle. I put the glasses to my eyes and watched in fascination as it glided along, supported by the currents, only occasionally needing to flap its wings to stay aloft. I could see no sign of a line hanging from the leg of the eagle.

I lowered the glasses. Maybe it wasn't Eddy, or maybe it was. Just because I couldn't see it didn't mean anything. Just like my Naani said, I shouldn't need proof, just faith when she said my grandfather had returned as an eagle. Somehow her stories made as much sense as anything else anybody had told me. And sometimes you have to close your eyes to open up your heart.

The eagle continued on its slow, circular path above my head. Even though I was alone … I didn't feel so lonely anymore.